S0-ATI-994

3 1833 04730 7123

Dear Reader,

It seems there are those people who glide through life. They're never at a loss for the right words, they've never had to diet, and they're immune to bad hair days. If you happen to be one of those super-perfect folks, stop reading now! I want you to go to your computer and drop me an e-mail, telling me how you do it. I'd gain a ton of shelf space if I could ditch my diet-of-the-week books.

As one of those thoroughly flawed souls, I'm intrigued by the idea of perfection. Is it really all it's cracked up to be? Actually, does it exist outside the pages of fashion magazines? *In Like Flynn*'s heroine, Annie Rutherford, is grappling with just these issues. Like me, she's pretty much given up on bodily perfection.

Okay, Dorien, but why an Irishman for a hot hero? Daniel Flynn is an exercise in self-indulgence, since I'm also seriously addicted to all things Irish. If you think I might be overstating the case, stop by www.dorienkelly.com and follow my dancing shamrocks!

Wishing you love, laughter and nearly perfect Irishmen!

Dorien Kelly

ROMANCE

NOV 1 7 2004

This guy was Pierce Brosnan's kid brother, not her boss's lost twin.

He said something to the blonde walking with him. She simpered in a way that Annie considered a slap in the face to all womankind. As they stepped off the airport escalator, she held her Flynn sign higher, practically daring Mr. Amazingly Gorgeous to be the missing Irishman.

Not surprisingly, he started walking her way. As he approached, Annie heard the easy Irish cadence of his speech and felt her stiff spine begin to relax as she was drawn to him.

She was going to marginalize this man?

Annie dug deep to embrace her inner bitch, who she knew had to be in residence even on non-PMS days. After ordering the traitorous shrew within to can the sighing and mewling, Annie Rutherford got down to business. She had a man to handle.

Dorien Kelly

In Like Flynn

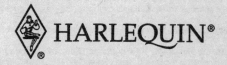

HARLEQUIN®

TORONTO • NEW YORK • LONDON
AMSTERDAM • PARIS • SYDNEY • HAMBURG
STOCKHOLM • ATHENS • TOKYO • MILAN • MADRID
PRAGUE • WARSAW • BUDAPEST • AUCKLAND

If you purchased this book without a cover you should be aware
that this book is stolen property. It was reported as "unsold and
destroyed" to the publisher, and neither the author nor the
publisher has received any payment for this "stripped book."

ISBN 0-373-44201-7

IN LIKE FLYNN

Copyright © 2004 by Dorien Kelly.

All rights reserved. Except for use in any review, the reproduction or
utilization of this work in whole or in part in any form by any electronic,
mechanical or other means, now known or hereafter invented, including
xerography, photocopying and recording, or in any information storage
or retrieval system, is forbidden without the written permission of the
publisher, Harlequin Enterprises Limited, 225 Duncan Mill Road,
Don Mills, Ontario, Canada M3B 3K9.

All characters in this book have no existence outside the imagination of
the author and have no relation whatsoever to anyone bearing the same
name or names. They are not even distantly inspired by any individual
known or unknown to the author, and all incidents are pure invention.

This edition published by arrangement with Harlequin Books S.A.

® and TM are trademarks of the publisher. Trademarks indicated with
® are registered in the United States Patent and Trademark Office, the
Canadian Trade Marks Office and in other countries.

Visit us at www.eHarlequin.com

Printed in U.S.A.

ABOUT THE AUTHOR

RITA® Award-nominated author Dorien Kelly is a former attorney who is much happier as an author. In addition to her years practicing business law, at one point or another she has also been a waitress, a law school teaching assistant and a professional chauffeur to her three children. She won't shake that chauffeur job for another seven years...not that she's counting.

When Dorien isn't writing or driving her kids around, she loves to travel, dabble in gourmet cooking and avoid doing the laundry. Winner of the Romance Writers of America's Golden Heart Award and the Georgia Romance Writers' Maggie Award, she lives in Michigan with her husband, children and two incredibly spoiled West Highland White Terriers named Ceili and Seamus.

Books by Dorien Kelly

Don't miss any of our special offers. Write to us at the following address for information on our newest releases.

Harlequin Reader Service
U.S.: 3010 Walden Ave., P.O. Box 1325, Buffalo, NY 14269
Canadian: P.O. Box 609, Fort Erie, Ont. L2A 5X3

1

Ann Arbor, Michigan

ANNIE RUTHERFORD always carried an extra five—okay, nine—pounds as though they were her insurance policy against quick starvation. That being said, she still couldn't fill out the top of her sister's best black cocktail dress. The bottom, unfortunately, was another story.

"Are you okay in there?" Elizabeth, her perfect elder sister, called from the other side of the bathroom door.

"I'm fine…just admiring the scenery," Annie replied. And what scenery it was.

Elizabeth, a Harvard business grad who made major cash in the fast world of finance, lived in a gorgeous renovated Victorian on the fringes of the University of Michigan's central campus. Her bathroom boasted French limestone floors, a steam shower large enough to host rainforest refugees, and a three-way mirror that amplified Annie's attributes to a fault. Since she wasn't a sucker for punishment, Annie averted her eyes.

"So does the dress fit?" her sister asked.

"Parts," she hedged. The length, for example, was perfect. At least her hips and rear made up for the difference between Elizabeth's five foot seven and her more pedestrian five foot five.

"Come on, let me in."

Annie surrendered to the inevitable. Endowed Elizabeth entered, strolled an assessing circle around Annie, then stood beside her.

"Maybe a gel bra," she suggested.

Annie met her sister's matching gray gaze in the mirror. "Yeah, like a quart on each side. And what about the bottom half?"

A slight frown settled between Elizabeth's brows. "It's not that bad…nothing a good foundation garment wouldn't fix."

Now there was a thought to put a girl off her food. Maybe a girdle, or whatever, would thrill an eighty-nine-year-old named Tilda, but the hell if Annie would consider it.

"I think I'll just hit the stores for something in my size."

Elizabeth sighed. They both knew Annie couldn't afford anything as elegant as Prada on her own. "I still think this could work. You've got a few days to straighten out the details."

"Too bad we can't just move my butt to my boobs," she said, then ignored Elizabeth's talk of "a consistent exercise program."

Generally, Annie was no slave to fashion, but the company cocktail party she'd be attending on Friday merited a raid on her sister's glamorous wardrobe. Word was that Hal Donovan, who had just returned from a month-long vacation in Ireland, planned to make a big announcement.

Hal was the elderly—but definitely not old—chairman of Donovan Enterprises, the parent company of Donovan's Wood-Fired Pizza. When Annie joined the Donovan empire fresh out of her not-quite-Harvard graduate school program, Hal had taken a liking to her and stepped in as her mentor. After months of drifting, she had discovered that she possessed a surprising gift for forecasting and interpreting trends. Not that this crystal-ball talent did anything for her on a personal level.

At least she was vice president of long-range planning and the only non-Donovan in the company's upper management. She had a great title and business cards to die for, but much to her regret, Donovan's had already conquered its market. Her job was a fast trip to nowhere.

Given Hal's fondness for nepotism, unless she married a Donovan—which was unlikely since the only single, nonjailbait one left was Annie's best friend Sasha, and she just didn't feel *that way* about her—Annie had reached the top of the ladder.

Maxing out at twenty-nine was unacceptable for a member of the Rutherford clan. Even Annie's brother, Sam, the family nonconformist, had quit his band, followed an accelerated track and finished his doctoral studies in archaeology, then quickly snagged an associate professor's position at a small college in Maine. All of which in Annie's estimation made him a total show-off.

Since she was now officially the lone, clueless Rutherford, she had been working late into the night on an idea that would make her résumé as sleek as her sister's dress—when her sister was wearing it, she amended, taking another glance in the mirror.

"Look, I can understand why you're excited about this party," Elizabeth said, "but from the stories you've told me, it sounds like old Hal can be—"

"Arbitrary? Quixotic?" Hal had grown a corner pizza shop into the largest privately owned carry-out and restaurant chain in the country. Annie figured he was entitled to be imperious.

Elizabeth nodded, then began to fuss with Annie's uncooperative hair, dragging it into a knot atop her head. "Don't get your hopes up. It's just as likely that his announcement won't be about your overseas franchise proposal."

Annie shooed her sister's hands away and stuck her hair behind her ears. She had slaved nearly every night for over six months on that franchise plan and figured it might well be her only shot at the big time. When she'd finished her proposal, she'd asked Elizabeth to vet it. For once, she'd received nothing more than a "great work" in response from her brilliant—and critical—sister.

If Annie had her way, Donovan's would set up company-owned outlets in airports and train stations throughout Europe. Once their product was familiar to consumers, the organization would step into phase two and sell franchises. If the idea worked in Europe, next they could tackle Asia. Major exposure without major expansion in Donovan's staff levels was a no-brainer.

She'd pitched the idea to Hal right before he'd left at the beginning of May to explore his roots. He'd seemed enthused. Or at least Annie chose to think he had.

"I have to get my hopes up," she said to her sister. "That's what life's all about, right? Besides, Sasha managed to pry loose from Hal that I'd be 'damn pleased' with his announcement. A guy wouldn't lie to his own granddaughter, would he?"

Of course, Hal wasn't exactly fond of Sasha, which added a kind of troubling dynamic. Annie pushed aside doubt and struggled with the dress's zipper. It had stuck at an annoying midshoulder-blade spot that only a contortionist could reach.

Elizabeth brushed aside Annie's hand and eased

down the zipper. "It's a solid business plan. No matter what happens, you should be proud of it."

Which was easy for Elizabeth to say.

"Thanks, but if it's totally unproven, it does nothing for my résumé. Manhattan calls, and I need to be shopping myself with headhunters before I hit thirty. It's just going to get tougher after that."

"Relax," her sister said. "Turning thirty means nothing. You have years to prove yourself."

Again, easy words from Elizabeth, who never failed to excel. Annie, on the other hand, always scrabbled on the lower reaches of "almost outstanding." Just once, she wanted to cling to the pinnacle. And she was determined to do it in the center of the business universe— New York City. She would move there, settle in, then never have to pack her belongings again. But without the international franchise deal up and running, she suspected she'd be lucky to hire in as a bottom-rung research grunt, let alone in the consultant's role she craved.

Distracted, she began to peel off the dress, then paused. She really didn't need to share every padded curve with her sister. Luckily, the phone rang.

Elizabeth glanced at her watch. "It's almost seven, so that has to be Gordon's nightly call," her sister said, referring to her rich and handsome long-distance boyfriend. "He wants to fly me to London this weekend. I wish it wasn't Mom and Dad's anniversary dinner...not that I could take the time from work, anyway."

Elizabeth rushed from the room, fleet on the wings of lust or love or whatever it was she felt for this guy she seldom saw.

Annie managed not to roll her eyes. She adored her

sister, but it was depressing to be related to her. "Round-the-world popularity. Such a tragedy."

Clifden, County Galway, Ireland

MIDNIGHT NEARED. Daniel Flynn drew deeply on his final cigarette, as would any condemned man. And as was the case with most poor, doomed bastards, he'd brought fate upon his own head. He tipped back his head and slowly expelled the smoke, savoring this final moment.

Finished, he stubbed the cigarette butt in an ashtray on the brown wooden pub table and made a silent vow that this truly would be his last smoke. Of course, that particular vow was well oiled, having been used more times than Daniel could count. Around him, friends and family laughed, sang and drank, always game for another party at Flynn's Pub.

He loved this place, truly he did. It was peat-smoke scented, dimly lit, warm and comfortable, even more home than the house down the street where he'd grown up. Daniel tried to summon a decent level of enthusiasm for the celebration surrounding him, when all he wanted was to escape to his flat above the pub. This fest in his honor was sitting nearly as poorly as was the thought of no more cigarettes.

Thailand and Tibet had been grand adventures, last year's autumn in Tuscany none too hard to take, but eight weeks in America? Agreeing to anything more than a month had made him a victim of his own bloody greed. To him, America was much like an amusement park. All the brash attitude and excitement were entertaining for a time, but then he found himself weary and looking for a hole to hide in.

"To Daniel," bellowed his brother James over the noise of the crowd, "may you find all the American women you want, and may they not find you wanting."

Daniel gave a sketchy smile and raised his pint glass in response. This trip was about refilling his bank account and nothing more. He didn't regret for an instant offering up his life savings to help rebuild the family pub after last year's fire. Still, a man needed to eat. He absently reached for his cigarette pack, found it empty, then recalled the vow he'd made seconds earlier. Aye, a man needed to eat...and not to smoke.

Just then, Aislinn O'Connell grabbed him by the hand and urged him up from his seat.

"One last dance," she said, "to tide me over till you come home again."

They'd no sooner cleared the tables and stools from the center of the small area than the music changed from hard-driving radio tunes to live music—a slow air, cloyingly sweet and romantic. Since he could hardly walk away, he took Aislinn in his arms and shot a glare at his other brother, Seán, on the fiddle, who laughed in reply.

Neither of Daniel's brothers understood his need to wander. They could see no purpose in traveling farther than the few hours from their town, across the boggy green landscape of Connemara, to Galway. And all in the family had hoped that one day he'd marry Aislinn. True, they'd once been lovers, but it had never been serious for either of them. She would not venture out of Ireland, and though he always came home, Daniel would not stay.

"So two months this time, is it? And during tourist season, yet," Aislinn said as they danced to the old melody.

"It was too good an offer to turn down." He was sure that his mam—always on the lookout for a good meddle—had already given Aislinn the financial particulars down to the last jingle of pocket change.

"Are you not worried that old man Donovan's mad?"

Daniel shrugged. "You met him during his visit. He's opinionated, to be sure, but not mad."

"Anyone offering his kind of money should be locked away."

"And here I thought you knew my value," he teased.

Aislinn laughed. "I do. That's why I'm thinking he's mad."

He squeezed her tightly to him for moment, an affectionate hug for an old friend. Aislinn's expression grew serious.

"What would have been wrong with staying for at least one summer?" she asked. "It's not as though your family couldn't use an extra hand. And of course there's that book you need to be writing."

"I've got conscience enough already." Not to mention sufficient guilt being heaped on him by his mam and da, who were currently snapping pictures of the party as though it might be the last Flynn's Pub would ever see.

He glanced again at Seán and James, and wondered how he, too, could be so strongly stamped a Flynn, with the family's height, dark hair and the Flynn blue eyes, yet not be a Flynn at the same time. This much he knew—the life of a full-time publican wasn't for him.

The fiddle music stopped, and over the applause one brother or another bellowed, "Give the girl a kiss, you fool."

Aislinn flicked back a lock of her curly brown hair, called a tart "kiss yourself" to his brothers, then said to Daniel, "I'd make it worth your while if you'd take those two eejits with you."

"You'd do better at getting me to stay here."

"And that would be so bad?"

He shook his head. "Leave it be, Aislinn."

To his brothers' loud hoots, she rose on tiptoe and gave him a kiss that tasted of resignation. "We'll all be missing you, Daniel."

"And I'll be missing you."

But even as he spoke, his heart began to drum with rising excitement, a reaction that thrilled him none too much. He truly was one sad-arsed addict. Even a voyage he had no real desire to take was enough to prime him.

As he walked Aislinn back to the bar and his fool brothers, he wondered what he would do when he grew too old to wander. Perhaps one day, in someplace he couldn't yet imagine, he'd find whatever it was that drove him. Maybe even in this Ann Arbor he'd consigned himself to.

And that wild thought gave Daniel Flynn his greatest laugh of the night.

Ann Arbor, Michigan

FOUR DAYS LATER, Annie removed her sister's black Prada cocktail dress from sentinel duty at the refrigerator door, where it had stood as a reminder of why she'd opted to starve herself. The good news was that she'd lost three pounds. Four, if she exhaled and put more weight on her right foot than her left while standing on the scale. The bad news—after a couple of glasses of water, it would all be back. Such was her evil, betraying metabolism.

Dress in hand, she padded her way through her condo, ignoring the box of extraneous stuff she had readied for the local donation drop box. No matter that

the NYC move was far off and far from a sure thing, it
never hurt to prepare.

Once in her bedroom, she slipped on the dress and
sucked in her breath while zipping. Thanks to super-
elastic pantyhose that came perilously close to Elizabeth's dreaded "foundation garment," plus a gel bra
that was a feat of engineering, the dress nearly fit. With
the rearrangement of her internal organs, breathing was
going to be a dicey thing, but breathing was overrated,
anyway.

Annie turned sideways and examined herself in the
mirror by her walk-in closet.

"Not bad," she murmured.

If she could survive this evening's cocktail party
without fainting from hunger, she had it made. And if
she did pass out, with luck Sasha would be at her side.
Others among her co-workers would roll her inert body
beneath a potted palm and rejoice. Being chairman's
pet was no more socially beneficial than it had been
back in fifth grade when she'd been teacher's pet. Still,
it paid better than the teacher's pet gig.

Annie applied her makeup, crammed her cell phone
and lipstick into a tiny excuse for a purse and hit the
road. As she traveled toward the sunset, Ann Arbor
proper gave way to suburb, which quickly thinned to
farmland. The drive was familiar. As part of upper management, she'd been to the Washtenaw Open Hunt Club
for company gatherings many times before.

Annie hadn't led a sheltered life. With professors for
parents, she and her siblings had lived in Japan and
traveled throughout Europe as extra baggage during
their parents' countless guest lecturer stints. Still, for all
she had seen, something about the Hunt Club's bizarre

mock antebellum opulence always left her feeling edgy. And that was the last thing she wanted right now. She needed to be *on, hot, dynamic*…in sum, not your standard Annie.

She pulled her car to the peak of the circular drive in front of the ersatz Tara's broad steps. The valet opened her car door, and Annie exited as smoothly as she could, given the constrictor-grip of her dress. Once standing, she wriggled the garment to its intended level and ignored the valet's grin. She ascended the stairs, did her best to shake off her case of the creeps, then readied to seize her future.

Sasha stood just inside the open French doors to the ballroom. She handed Annie a glass of white wine. "It's a decent chardonnay. Drink up so we can get another in before Gramps has the bar haul out the cheap stuff."

Annie wasn't surprised at her friend's party-down attitude, which was totally at odds with her appearance. Sasha was small, ivory-skinned, black-haired and incredibly slender—almost a pen-and-ink of a woman. Yet beneath that ascetic exterior lurked a metabolism in overdrive. As Donovan's head of community relations, she recreated with more enthusiasm and slept less than anyone Annie had ever known. Annie was content to draft behind her like the second-place driver in a grand prix.

"Here's to good news," Sasha said, raising her glass.

They toasted each other, downed healthy swallows, then pinned on matching corporate smiles and made their way into the throng.

Beneath the soft piano music, an undercurrent of anticipation hummed through the room. Then again, it might have been only in Annie's head. She took another nervous sip of wine. The chilly liquid hit the bottom of her empty stomach.

As she glanced around, she noticed that a screen had been set up at the far end of the room. On it flashed photographs of crumbling stone towers, towering gray cliffs and whitewashed cottages, all set in a green and rocky landscape. Photos from Hal Donovan's vacation, no doubt. Annie frowned. Sure, Hal could be a little odd, but he'd never held his employees hostage for a travelogue before. She took another swallow of smooth chardonnay as insulation against any upcoming lectures on leprechauns.

Hal stood nearly straight ahead, deep in conversation with Richard and Duane, two of his four sons involved in the family business, neither of whom looked happy. Of course, Donovans generally looked unhappy when in one another's company. Not a whole lot of conversation took place. Mostly, Hal ordered his sons around, and they silently seethed with resentment, all of which made for some peachy management meetings.

As though they sensed her watching, Richard and Duane shot stern looks her way. She told herself that it wasn't about the franchise deal, that she shouldn't overanalyze what she saw, but that was pretty much like telling herself that a chocolate bar didn't help PMS. She gulped the rest of her wine and thought nothing of it when Sasha handed her another.

One drink usually smoothed the edge off her nerves, but already Annie surfed a serious buzz. Food was necessary. While Sasha and she made nice to the guys on the corporate legal staff—who were people you didn't want to cross—Annie tracked the progress of a scarlet-coated waiter headed in her direction. Whatever this guy was serving smelled like heaven, Annie-style—lots of garlic and butter. Ignoring the conversation buzzing around her, she willed him closer.

Annie and the waiter made eye contact. *Just two steps more, buddy, and you're mine.*

As was the case with Annie and most guys, his attention strayed. He wandered to her left. She concentrated harder.

This way. R-i-i-i-ght here.

Time was seriously of the essence since his tray was nearly empty. She reached out a hand. Her mouth began to water. Just then, Sasha stepped in and took the last item.

"Shrimp scampi," she said to Annie over a full mouth. "Primo."

"Great."

The waiter retreated. Annie felt a tragic emptiness second only to her brief New Year's try at a carb-free diet. Well, hell, at least she had her wine to tide her over.

After another swig she said to Sasha, "I'll be back. It's time to stalk a waiter."

She was about to turn away when a rusty-with-hard-living-and-whiskey voice came over the sound system.

"Glad you could all make it," Hal Donovan said. Annie spotted the stocky older man at a podium near the grand piano.

"Better hang on," Sasha murmured, briefly closing her fingers around Annie's wrist.

Annie stilled. At least, that's how it looked from the outside. Inside was another jangled, stressed reality altogether.

"I'm sure some of you thought that I'd brought you here tonight so I could announce my retirement. A few of you were probably even praying for it," he added with a disgruntled glance at his sons standing in a row.

"Earlier this year, you might have been right. Then about a month ago, I had a visit from our vice president of long-range planning."

Sasha elbowed Annie. Had her glass not been nearly empty, she would have been wearing its contents.

"This is it," Sasha whispered.

Annie noted in an abstract sort of way that the vice president of long-range planning had suddenly begun to feel a little dizzy. She focused on Hal, ignoring the daggers coming from nearby, where Rachel, her main competition at Donovan Enterprises, stood.

"Annie's enthusiasm was contagious. She urged me to look at our business in a new way...not to rest on past successes. As you all know, I'm not much for listening to anybody, but I've begun to think she has a point. It's time for Donovan Enterprises to become vital...hungry..."

Annie's heart began to dance double-time. This wasn't dizziness—she was giddy.

"We're going to expand...reach for new horizons..."

She grabbed hold of Sasha's hand and shot a lip curl toward Rachel, who was already sending Annie a pretty good one, too. For once, life was happening exactly as Annie had scripted it. Rachel was yesterday's news.

"Breathe!" Sasha hissed.

"Donovan is a name that will soon be known..."

Throughout Europe, Annie silently prompted, gripping tighter to Sasha.

"...for its chain of Irish pubs across the country."

Holy crap. Somebody had seriously jacked with Hal's copy of the script. The one breath that Annie had managed to draw slowly hissed out, leaving her deflated.

Hal raised his whiskey glass and said, "To Annie

Rutherford, for reminding me that there are still mountains to climb."

Close, but no big, fat, stinkin' Hal-type cigar. She'd meant the Alps, not the Rockies.

Sasha again planted her elbow in Annie's ribs. "Raise your glass," she ordered out of the side of her mouth. "Now."

Annie did. At least, she was pretty sure she did.

"If she agrees," Hal said, then gave a brief and-how-could-she-not? chuckle, "Annie will be spearheading this new venture. Let's cheer her on!"

On cue, the pianist began to play something that sounded vaguely *Riverdance*ish. Annie watched in utter, dry-mouthed disbelief as a bunch of kids in blindingly loud embroidered velvet dresses danced their way into the room.

Sasha took her empty wineglass. "Let me get you a refill. You're going to need it."

Sasha might as well bring a damn case of wine. While putting together her proposal, Annie had survived six months of no movies, no fun, no friends and definitely no dates worth mentioning, and what did she have to show for it? Zip. And Hal was about to gamble a whole lot of money—not to mention her career—that he could succeed in a corner of the industry that was notorious for making bankruptcy attorneys fat, happy and well paid.

Annie shook hands and chatted with well-wishers and some clearly not-so well-wishers. Her face began to ache from her manufactured isn't-life-wonderful? expression. She also had the eerie sensation that somebody other than she was making her lips move and platitudes come out. She hoped her responses sounded a whole lot more polite than "I'm so totally screwed," which was reeling in her head. Her script had tanked, but a lot of these guys would kill for the opportunity she'd just been handed.

Hal stopped by long enough to issue marching orders. "Meet me at the office tomorrow morning at eight. And smile, Annie. This is supposed to be fun."

Fun?

She took it all back, every kind word, every charitable thought. Hal Donovan was quite possibly insane. But she also owed him her loyalty, which meant that on a Saturday morning when she intended to be vilely hungover, she would be there for him.

She worked up a feeble smile. "Okay, Hal."

He laughed. "See if you can produce something a little more convincing before tomorrow."

And then he left her standing alone in a sea of people, none of whom, she was sure, could feel any more miserable than she. All was not lost, though. Her faithless waiter had reappeared. Annie took the offered cocktail fork and plate, then speared a bacon-wrapped scallop from the tray. The waiter readied to move on, but Annie had serious plans to blow out the seams of her sister's cursed cocktail dress.

"Settle in, Ned," she said, reading the name on the guy's black plastic name tag. "You and I aren't going anywhere."

2

In an ideal world, a woman would never have to go to the office on a Saturday. Of course, in an ideal world, neither would she have ended Friday night depressed and overdressed at Fraser's Pub—which, thank God, had nothing Irish about it. There, Annie had swilled beer to top off the two pounds of scallops and bacon she'd already inhaled.

Sasha had humored her right up until the Jell-O shot challenge she'd issued to a women's softball team. Annie had been certain she and Sasha could take them, but then again, she'd also been certain that today she'd be mapping out a franchise time line. Her judgment was clearly suspect.

After taking Annie back to her car this morning, Sasha had followed her downtown to headquarters. She was now perched on Annie's desk, trying to provide moral support and additional calories.

"Come on, just one little bite," Sasha wheedled, waving a doughnut under Annie's nose. "It's cream-filled."

Annie took the doughnut, sucked out the guts, then handed her friend the carcass. "Happy?"

Sasha dropped it into the wastebasket beside Annie's desk. "Now I am."

At least someone was.

Annie settled forehead-down on her desk, her arms cradling her head. The wood felt cool and soothing— a scallop, beer and emotion overdose wasn't easily overcome.

"This isn't like you," Sasha said. "You need to get a grip. Just because Gramps is distracted doesn't mean your proposal's dead."

"I know."

"Then don't take this so hard, okay? You're making me want to cry."

"I'm not crying."

"Yeah, but you have been."

Annie turned her head just enough to peer at her friend out of one eye.

"Only in the shower and that doesn't count. It's like eating over the sink."

Sasha frowned, obviously trying to work her way through Annie's twisted logic. Annie was pleased for the distraction. She had never discussed her endgame— leaving the Donovan fold—with Sasha. It didn't seem right to place her best friend in a position where she'd be pulled between competing loyalties.

The phone rang. Annie sent one hand venturing for it, but then heard Sasha's crisp voice saying, "Ms. Rtherford's office. Oh, hi, Gramps. Sure, I'll tell her you're ready."

As Sasha hung up, Annie rose from her workplace version of the fetal position. Sasha stood, too, and gave her a brief hug, which seemed to draw at least some of the dejection from her bones.

"I'd better get this over with," she said.

"Want me to stay?" Sasha offered.

"Nah...I'm fine."

Sasha, smart girl that she was, took Annie at her word and walked her to the elevator. Annie pushed the up button and Sasha the Down, which felt ass-backward to Annie.

Before she was ready, Annie was exiting at the top floor. At the end of the thickly carpeted reception area, the door to Hal's office was open, yet not exactly accessible. Even on a Saturday, his secretary, Mrs. D'Onfrio, sat at her post, silver hair perfectly coiffed and guardian-of-the-nest expression sharply in place. Annie knew it was improbable that Mrs. D'Onfrio lacked a first name, but she'd also never met anyone who knew it. She'd never even heard Hal use it.

"Good morning, Mrs. D.," Annie offered.

Mrs. D. looked her up and down from over the tops of her reading glasses, and then gave a rueful shake of her head. "You go on in. I'll bring coffee."

Annie stepped inside. "Good morning, Hal." He was dressed in riding garb, as if he was channeling Scarlett O'Hara's dad. A brown-and-yellow hound-stooth jacket was possibly not the best fashion statement on a man wider than he was tall, but who was she to comment?

"Annie, take a look at these."

He rounded his desk and handed her a stack of photographs. Annie thumbed through them. *Pub…pub…donkey in field…flowers…pub with old dude behind the bar…castle…pub…pub…* Okay, she could see the genesis of Hal's current fixation.

When she was done checking out the snapshots, she looked up to find Mrs. D., who took the pics, handed Annie a mug of coffee with two teaspoons of sugar, exactly as Annie liked, then disappeared.

"You've had a night to think about my offer," Hal said, then eased his bulk into his worn leather chair. "What do you say?"

She sat opposite him and cupped her mug in both hands. "I was pretty sure that no wasn't an option."

"And if it were?"

Annie sighed. How could she explain to the man that he was offering her up for career suicide? She knew nothing about the mechanics of restaurant start-ups. "I'm grateful for everything you've taught me. You've given me huge opportunities, and—"

"I've given you opportunities because you're smart. It was as much to my advantage as yours. And now I'm giving you something new to try. You've been in a rut, Annie, not at all yourself."

Annie couldn't disagree. She'd been sleepless and stressed from trying to do her day job plus find time to work on her poor, dead franchise proposal, but that wasn't her boss's problem.

"Hal, your idea is dangerous. Half of all restaurants fail within the first year, and very few ever hit the five-year mark. The odds get even worse when you pick a specialized niche like Irish pubs."

He grinned. "Lies, damn lies and statistics. I'm a gambler and I know what I'm doing. Look at the years of experience we have here at Donovan's."

"The pizza business is different. Your restaurants get a boost off your carry-out business. There's no synergy with a pub concept."

Hal snorted. "Synergy. That's one hell of a word. Save it for a fancier audience, huh?"

Annie took a diplomatic sip of her coffee. It didn't sit well atop the doughnut guts.

"Annie, I'm not doing this blind. I have a secret weapon. He'll be at the airport in just a few hours."

The knot in her stomach grew tighter. *"He?"*

Hal pulled a cigar from his mahogany desktop humidor. As he rolled it between his fingers, he said, "His name is Daniel Flynn. He's been in the pub business for decades."

Great. Some old Irish coot.

"You'll like him…everybody does. I've hired him on a sixty-day consulting contract. He'll give us the authentic touch those bullsh—those, uh, other places don't have."

Like a drunk in every corner.

Hal's bark of laughter rang through the posh office. "Did you just roll your eyes, Annie Rutherford?"

"No." Something about the way he treated her seemed to bring out childish behavior, including this lie.

"I know you wanted to run with the overseas idea, and once you've launched my pub chain, we'll really hash it over."

That, at least, was a reprieve.

"I'm not asking for a lifetime," Hal continued. "Give me three months. And in those three months, I want action, Annie. I want the first pub here in Ann Arbor and I want it open in time for the start of football season."

If wanting to barf counted as action, she was seriously there. His schedule would have made sense if they'd begun six months earlier. Thanks to the tradition of University of Michigan football, on home game Saturdays Ann Arbor's streets teemed with one hundred thousand additional people, all thirsty, hungry and out to have too good of a time. But it was already early June and they had no site or plan. In fact they had nothing but Hal's faith-and-begorra fantasy. She was determined to be a one-woman intervention.

"What about a liquor license?" she asked, thankfully aware that months might pass before one would be granted.

"We'll convert the State Street Donovan's."

"What?" The central campus landmark had been his first sit-down restaurant and still ranked among the company's best performers.

"That saves us the trouble of the liquor license since we've already got one. We're shaking things up, you included. This is your baby. I've told Richard and the boys that it's hands-off as far as they're concerned. We're doing this on a need-to-know basis, and they don't need to."

Dandy. Now she'd been placed smack in the middle of the Donovan generational conflict. Hal might as well hand her a shovel and tell her to dig her own grave.

"If you want to try to argue me out of this, do it on Monday," Hal said. "Right now, Flynn's on his way from New York. I want you to head to Metro and pick him up. Mrs. D. has the flight details."

"You want *me* to get him? Like a chauffeur?"

Hal chuckled. "Damn undemocratic response, Annie. This is no different than the month I had you spend in front of the pizza oven."

"But that was about learning the business!"

"Sure was," he replied as he stowed his cigar into a fancy leather carrying case, then tucked it into his jacket's breast pocket. "Think of yourself as Flynn's welcoming committee."

"Right." She preferred to imagine herself waving a farewell hankie and getting on with her life. When she returned to her office, she'd do both this Flynn and herself a favor and call him a limo. She stood. "I'll see you on Monday, Hal."

She was nearly to the door when Hal's voice brought her up short. "No delegating."

"But—"

"Humor me."

So when was someone going to humor her?

ABOUT AN HOUR LATER, Annie stood along the fringe of the McNamara Terminal's baggage-claim area. Her purse was slung over her shoulder, and she held a sign labeled Flynn in one hand and the remains of a bag of pretzels in the other. As designated gofer, she'd sunk low, but what gave her an uncontrollable case of the munchies was the thought that this moment might be the high point of the next three months.

Hal Donovan's idea of a "secret weapon" scared the hell out of her. If he had retained a top restaurant consultant…great! She would have tagged behind the demigod and learned all she could. But even decades behind the bar had nothing to do with big business.

She didn't want to see Hal get conned or his concept fail. True, it was Hal's money and Hal's project and maybe she shouldn't be taking it so much to heart. Problem was, it would be easier to stop stress eating than it would be to give less than her all.

On the drive to Metro Airport, she'd already decided to marginalize the Irishman. She'd provide him with a nice desk, a phone and lots of make-work. Then she'd do what countless other businesspeople and politicians did—she'd cloak her lack of knowledge with a top-notch team and deliver Hal's pub chain the launch it deserved. She had no other choice.

Temporarily tucking the sign under her arm, Annie finished off the last few broken pretzel bits. As she used her fingertip to gather the coarse salt from the bottom of the bag, she speculated on what this Flynn would look like. If he was the old guy from the snapshots she'd perused, she'd have no problem spotting him. She just needed to find Hal's secret twin, from whom he'd been separated at birth.

Activity picked up as travelers began to stream down the escalator. She quickly tossed the pretzel bag in the trash and held up her sign. Some likely suspects glanced her way, but all passed by. The crowd drifted toward the luggage carousel with the New York flight number showing on the sign above it.

Minutes passed, and traffic thinned. Annie folded the sign and tucked it into her purse, then retrieved her phone and dialed Mrs. D.

Hal's secretary said that there had been no messages from Mr. Flynn and didn't Annie think that she'd have contacted her if there were? Duly reprimanded, Annie settled in at one of the clusters of plastic seats and watched loving couples, weary businessmen and families with whiny kids get on with their lives.

Lucky buggers.

At the far end of the area, the escalator hummed, empty of passengers. In time, only a few stragglers, some redcaps and the lost luggage guy were there to keep Annie company. Just when she was readying to send out a Flynn search team, another group rode down the escalator. Ever hopeful, Annie stood and walked toward them, hastily pulling the crumpled Flynn sign from her purse.

The first two of the group were women in flowing

robes and veils—clearly not Flynn. Next was a man with a half-dressed blonde clinging to his arm. J.Lo at an awards ceremony had nothing on this female. Annie skipped all the cleavage and focused on the guy.

He was tall…make that tall, dark-haired and arrogantly handsome. He wasn't dressed to thrill, yet he made a pair of blue jeans and a white button-down shirt look like art. Over his free shoulder was slung a laptop computer in its black travel bag, and he held a blue jacket or sweatshirt or something in that hand.

Annie was more interested in his face. This guy was Pierce Brosnan's kid brother, not Hal's lost twin. For him to be Flynn, with his decades of pub wisdom, he'd have to have started behind the bar as an infant.

He said something to the blonde. She simpered in a way that Annie considered a slap in the face to all womankind. Of course, no guy this good-looking had ever found the time of day for Annie. She was damn sure that even if one did, she wouldn't produce a heartbeat-from-an-orgasm squeal like blondie's. The guy smiled, almost as though he considered blondie's response his due.

The happy couple had begun to depress her on some visceral level that she was too hungover to think about. As they stepped off the escalator, then neared, she held the Flynn sign higher, practically daring Mr. Amazingly Gorgeous to be the missing Irishman.

At first, it seemed that he'd seen her and counted her as irrelevant to his perfect life. Then his gaze returned, and he smiled. He walked her way, blondie teetering along beside him in pointy shoes that had to kill her feet. As he approached, Annie heard the easy Irish cadence of his speech and felt her stiff spine begin to relax as she was drawn within his pull.

She was going to marginalize this man?

She dug deep to embrace her inner bitch, who she knew had to be in residence even on non-PMS days. After ordering the traitorous shrew within to can the sighing and mewling, Annie Rutherford got down to business. She had a man to handle.

FOUR OUT OF FIVE women generally liked Daniel, which made it lamentable that the fifth was standing before him. Even sadder was the fact that she was beautiful in a wholesome, wholly American way. Her shoulder-length hair was a shiny golden brown and her gray eyes would have been exceptionally fine had they not been narrowed with cold intent. Yes, he'd much rather have an unattractive woman hate him.

"You're Flynn?"

He winced at the way she said the name.

"Daniel Flynn. You'd be Annie?" he asked while trying to free his right arm from its current attachment. "Mrs. D'Onfrio told me to be expecting you." Once freed, he offered his hand for a shake.

She didn't seem to notice.

"I'm Ms. Rutherford," she said, stretching out the *Ms.* until it rode the air buzz-saw sharp. "And you're late."

She had that spot-on. He felt nearly dead. Even though his face already hurt from smiling, he offered another in hopes that it would force one from her.

"A bit of a problem getting off the plane is all," he said.

April, his bit of extra baggage, cut in. "He's a hero! I started choking, and he saved me! You should have seen it! It was—"

"Nothing," he said. "No more than anyone else would have done."

He'd been seated at the very back of the plane—no place for a quiet rest, which he sorely needed. Always game to renew acquaintances, Daniel had arrived in America a few days prior to the start of his new job. His Manhattan friends had done their best to murder him by sleep deprivation, and as it happened, having an aircraft engine directly behind his head today wasn't to be the last of his suffering.

As he'd waited his turn to exit the aircraft, April had been standing in front of him, tossing down hard candies as though they'd be confiscated at the door. When she'd grabbed her throat with one hand and waved the other about, Daniel had gotten her into position and heaved the air—and sweets—right out of her.

He supposed he should be buoyed by his good deed. Instead, he was weary and feeling oddly alone. He didn't deserve this enthusiasm from April, and though he'd been raised to be polite, his manners were wearing thin.

He needn't have worried about undue adulation from Ms. Rutherford, though. She was now scowling at the bags lined up near the sleeping luggage carousel.

"Those are yours?"

"Not the lavender monogrammed ones." Those, he'd wager, were vapid April's.

"Then get them and let's go."

"I've apologized for being late. Is there something else bothering you?" Daniel watched as expressions flitted across her face. She was an easy read, this unhappy American.

"I hate airports," she finally said, but Daniel knew his name could have just as neatly filled in that blank.

After he'd gathered his bags and said goodbye to his

new friend—collecting an unwanted offer in the process—he decided to give it one more try.

"So," he said as they walked toward the escalator, "we'll be working together, I've been told. Have you known Hal long?"

"Professionally, five years."

"And you've experience in the bar business?" he asked as they ascended.

"None," she said, then strode on to the garage's automated payment machine.

None. And he thought this was to have been an easy bit of money. He dropped the bag in his right hand and felt his jacket pocket for a pack of smokes. There were none, of course. He'd have to make do with the memory of the one he'd cadged on the drive to the airport.

"Are you coming?" his escort prodded, her voice echoing into the largely empty space around them.

He'd been a fecking idiot, second only to his brothers, when he'd said yes to Hal. Daniel should have offered to come for a quick look-see, then decided if the job suited him. But here he was, and damned if he'd serve less than his sentence because one pretty American found him inconvenient.

"I don't suppose you smoke?" he asked, all the while knowing it was more likely that she worked in Amsterdam's red-light district on the weekend.

"It's unhealthy."

Ah, but the quitting was killing him.

They were in her car—which he found to be an intriguing mine of paper and files—and driving down the freeway before she pried loose any more words. "So where, exactly, am I taking you?"

After wrestling with the seat belt, Daniel pulled a

piece of paper from his pocket and unfolded it. "Six eighty-four Cobblestone Court."

She turned to stare at him, and the car swerved.

"Mind your lane," he yelped, leaning away from the massive truck now within touching distance.

She yanked the wheel in the opposite direction. After both of them had drawn ragged breaths, she said, "Let me get this straight. You said Cobblestone Court?"

"I did."

"And you'll be living there?"

He gave his answer carefully, timing it for a gap in traffic. "Yes."

A sweep of color rose on her cheeks. Daniel couldn't believe that he noticed it when he'd do better minding the road for her. Last year's Amazon trip was beginning to feel tame by comparison.

"This is some sort of joke, isn't it? Hal put you up to this."

He briefly closed his eyes, thinking of the bottle of aspirin just a few short feet behind him, buried in his suitcase.

"No joke," he said. "Just a place to sleep."

"Come on... Why don't you just tell me what's going on?"

"And here I was ready to ask the same of you," he said. "You first."

"Fine, then." Doing his best to ignore the sheer number of cars flying by—and the anger coming even closer—Daniel settled into his tale. "While he was visiting Ireland, Hal Donovan and I met up at my family's pub in Clifden. He liked the town, liked us, and we liked him, too, so he stayed a few weeks beyond what he'd planned. When he was leaving, he asked me if I'd be willing to lend a hand in a new business venture. I was, so here I am.

"As for where I'll be staying, since I've no love for sterile hotels, Mrs. D'Onfrio put me in contact with a rental agent. I looked at the files she sent me and decided to rent a town house on Cobblestone Court. It's no grand conspiracy to muck up your life, Ms. Rutherford. And now if you don't mind, I'll just close my eyes until we get there. Are you needing directions?" He waved the map he'd printed off the Internet.

She laughed, not that it sounded especially cheery. "No thanks. I live two doors down."

Aye, the Amazon and its serpents were sounding placid, indeed.

"Neighbors. Grand," he said, then feigned death.

3

ANNIE STOOD WITH the Irishman in the middle of a living room that exactly matched hers, except this one was empty, with not so much as an extra dust mote for company. Not good news, since she was in need of distraction.

She refused to meet his eyes and risk working up any humane feelings toward him. In some remote way, Annie recognized that she needed a behavior-modification device—maybe a fat rubber band around her wrist. She could snap it good and hard as a reminder that aiming her frustration at Flynn instead of Hal Donovan was bad. Unfortunately, she was rubber-band free. Beyond that, she'd already discovered that once she focused on the Irishman, it was unnaturally difficult to look away.

"I don't suppose there's a furniture truck coming?" she asked as she surveyed the freshly painted white walls and new buff-colored carpet.

"I'll be visiting a rental place on Monday."

For lack of any other focal point, she looked in his general direction as he set down two overstuffed bags, then slipped the strap of his laptop case from his shoulder. Her gaze was drawn upward as he stood taller.

Damn, he had the bluest eyes she'd ever seen. He scrutinized her, and as though he could sense her thoughts, his mouth quirked into a smile that did unacceptable things to her pulse. She needed to keep the upper hand, assuming she'd ever had it.

"Mrs. D'Onfrio gave me a list," he said. "She's good at that, isn't she?"

"The best." Annie glanced at her watch, since she'd already done the wall-and-floor thing. When she looked back, he was still watching her. She waited an instant to be sure she wasn't paranoid, but he kept looking. "Do I have crumbs on my face or something?"

"Freckles," he said, sounding surprised.

"Yeah, well…" To hide the blush she knew was coming, she walked toward the sliding glass door that led onto the small balcony, also exactly like hers. They shared the same view of green treetops, with Riverside Park downhill, only a block away.

He came to stand beside her. He was silent, a state she found almost as unsettling as his nearness. She worked up some tour-guide chat.

"They built the Cobblestone complex just a couple of years ago. Before that, it was all light industry around here, which was kind of a waste of a view. That's the Huron River," she said, pointing to the ribbon of gray-green just visible past the trees. "Downtown Ann Arbor is across the river and a little south. Behind us is the University Hospital complex."

The Irishman made some polite sound of interest, or maybe he yawned. Either way, her heart kept drumming at a humiliatingly quick pace.

"Along the river is a chain of parks and…"

And what? She was out of words, nearly empty of thought, except that she needed to escape, but her parents had raised her too damn well. Much as she wanted to ditch Daniel Flynn, guilt had shaped itself into a mile-high roadblock.

"Why don't I at least take you to a supermarket?" she blurted. "You need some food and, I dunno, stuff, I'm sure."

"A shower and sleep, mostly."

She edged toward the center of the room. "You don't even have a bed."

He gestured at the floor. "I've slept on worse."

That was territory she didn't want to explore. Not where he slept, or when, or whether he did it naked. Okay, so she was human. Even if he didn't exactly float her boat on a personal level, the naked concept deserved some consideration.

"Look, Ms. Rutherford—"

"You probably should call me Annie," she said, which was as close to charm as she could manage while quelling images of the Irishman stripped bare.

"Ms. Rutherford," he repeated firmly. "You've made it clear that you're none too glad to have me working with you, so if it's somehow bothering your conscience to leave me here, don't let it. You've done your duty, and I can find my way back should I venture out. Fair enough?"

Annie worked up the guts to really look at him. What she saw made her feel smaller than the time she was five and gave her sister's favorite Barbie a punk hairdo. He appeared tired, maybe a bit sad, and totally sick of her.

"Sure. Fair enough," she said, then turned to the door. "I'll see you in the office on Monday."

As Annie left Daniel Flynn alone in his empty home, all she could think was how guilt totally sucked. She walked the six steps from the stoop of Flynn's brick-

and-fieldstone town house with its garage tucked below, to the sidewalk, turned right and headed to her identical unit, too busy mentally flogging herself over her pissy attitude to look up. Then her progress was stopped by a roadblock even more solid than her guilt.

"Whoa, Annie. Watch where you're going," advised the second—or was that third?—unwelcome male of her day.

Through the glare of the noontime June sun, Annie squinted up at her next-door neighbor, who unfortunately was also her ex-boyfriend, Garth "the perpetual grad student" Walker.

"Sorry," she said automatically while backing from his grip. Once freed, she scowled at him, wondering how she had ever found his fake hippie act sexy. At least she'd never been stupid enough to fall in love with him. Viewing the whole mess in retrospect, admitting to lust was bad enough.

It had been months since she'd seen Garth—no mean feat considering they shared common walls. And not very thick ones, at that. While dating him, she'd discovered what a loser he was when his new roomie—brought in to cut costs—made it gasp-howl-and-pantingly clear that she and Garth had begun to share more than space. Annie didn't hold it against Screamer Mei as much as she did Garth. At least Mei had been right out there with her activities. Garth had played the moron card, claiming he had no clue why Mei would be screaming his name.

Annie's Garthless streak might be broken, but she planned to make this encounter mercifully brief. She danced a little sidestep to her right. He followed.

"Wanna let me by?" she asked.

The fact that he didn't move from the center of the sidewalk made it pretty clear he didn't.

"How are you?" His words oozed pity, the creep.

"Great." She tried a quick dodge in the opposite direction, but Garth was on to her.

"And your family?"

"Great, too. Anyone else you care to ask about or are you going to let me by?"

He reached out, and she knew that he was going to trace the freckles across her cheekbones, just as he used to.

"No touching," she warned, raising a hand to fend him off.

Garth frowned. "I thought maybe you were past the hard feelings."

Annie didn't believe in violence and was even less fond of impulse, which was why what she did next totally shocked her. She stamped square in the middle of the bastard's Birkenstock-clad foot. Garth's answering yowl brought immediate, bloodthirsty satisfaction.

"Think again, weasel boy," she said, then cruised to her own front door.

Of course, by the time she was alone in her kitchen, Mother Guilt had settled in for a return visit. She wasn't sure which packed the bigger punch—the justifiable Daniel Flynn guilt, or remorse for *not* feeling bad about Garth's flattened toes.

Annie wanted to crawl into bed, pull the covers up to her eyebrows and wait for a better day. However, hibernation required more food than the bag of pretzels and doughnut guts she'd eaten. Praying for starch and sugar, she opened her fridge.

"Crap." It was empty, of course. The freezer was equally pathetic—only a couple of ice trays and what was either a frost-encrusted boneless chicken breast or some kind of exotic fish fillet her parents had foisted on her.

Since she was doomed to return to the outside world, Annie decided she might as well have company. Sasha had already suffered enough this morning. It was Elizabeth's turn. She grabbed the phone and dialed her sister's number.

"Hey, what are you doing?" she asked when Elizabeth picked up. The question was a formality, since the answer seldom varied.

"Working," replied her sister.

Ah, the comfort of a constant in a sadly screwy world. "Want to take a break?"

"I really don't have the time."

"Aw, come on… You can meet me at Zingerman's." Annie had pulled out the big guns. Even a food snob like Elizabeth couldn't pass up Zingerman's Deli, with its endless array of imported everything.

"All right," her sister said after only the briefest of pauses. "We need to talk about what you're bringing for tomorrow's dinner, anyway."

"Dinner?"

"Mom…Dad…their anniversary?"

Double-shit-anchovy pizza. Annie screwed her eyes shut. "Uh…"

"Don't you read your e-mail or check your phone messages? We scheduled this weeks ago, Annie. I left you reminders." She gave an exasperated big-sister sigh that hurt like hell as it echoed in Annie's aching head. "I suppose you don't even have a gift, do you?"

Like she'd admit it. "Just meet me at Zingerman's, okay?"

Annie hung up. She brushed her teeth and swallowed a couple of aspirin, but still didn't feel right. She shucked her dress-nice-for-the-visitor white cotton sweater and khakis, then slipped into comfort clothes—her roomiest jeans and a soft and worn tee. Definitely an improvement.

The deli wasn't much more than a half mile from home, but she remained in no condition to consider walking. Actually, even on a good day, that was a no-go. She did make it to her car, allowing herself only a brief glance at the Irishman's place. He was probably asleep somewhere behind those bare windows, dreaming of an America free of hostile females.

A quick drive across the river brought Annie within deli distance. In the first certifiable miracle of the day, a parking space opened on the brick-paved street just as she approached. Annie was inside the tight confines of Zingerman's and had filled a basket with gourmet anniversary gift stuff from the selection stacked ceiling-high by the time Elizabeth arrived.

Her sister sighed when she spotted the basket. "Let me guess…"

"So it's not a personalized scrapbook or whatever, but who has time for that?"

Elizabeth's mouth took a superior tilt.

Back in the day, Annie should have chopped off the whole damn Barbie's head. "It was a rhetorical question, okay?"

She herded her sister to the deli side of the store, where they placed their orders. Elizabeth chose a calorie-friendly salad, while Annie felt proud that she'd managed not to ask for extra meat to go with her sandwich's double cheese. Elizabeth went outside to wait at a table for their order while Annie paid for her anniversary offering.

Once on the patio, Annie had to admire the perfect Ann Arbor afternoon. A soft breeze carried guitar music from someplace just out of sight, and customers from the nearby farmers' market wandered past, bags packed with organic spinach and honey and other healthy things never found in her home.

Their food arrived. Elizabeth toyed with her salad while Annie tried to open her mouth wide enough to encompass a half pound of fresh mozzarella and rosemary-edged ham.

"Any reason in particular that you chose to order something made for two?" Elizabeth asked after a sip of mineral water.

"Trust me, I could have ordered for four." She gave her sister a condensed version of last night's cocktail party, Hal's Mad Plan and the Irishman's arrival. Stomping on Garth seemed like a bush-league annoyance compared to all that.

Elizabeth set down her fork. "Your franchise proposal couldn't have been any tighter. I'm sorry, Annie. Really, I am."

Annie's eyes began to water. Damn sunshine.

"Yeah, I'm sorry, too." She peeled back the top of her sandwich and picked at the tomato. "All I need to do is hang on for three months. I'll give Hal his pub, then float my idea again." But just now, three months sounded like a life sentence.

"You know, you might not even need implementation of the franchise program on your résumé. If you're set on this New York move, I know some people who'd be worth talking to. We'll do some networking, okay?" Elizabeth offered.

While she wiped the tears from her lower lashes, Annie rethought the death-to-Lizzie's-Barbies concept.

"Thanks," she said. "I really do love you, you know?"

Elizabeth nearly winced, then quickly glanced around. She was probably scared that someone might have heard Annie's utterly un-Rutherford-like public admission of sisterly affection.

"Launching a pub might not be all bad," Elizabeth said after an uncomfortable pause.

Annie knew that was as close to an "I love you, too" as she'd be receiving. Even though she wasn't feeling especially rah-rah, she decided to pick up on her sister's cheerleading attempt.

"Sure, I figure there's no job you can't learn something from, even opening a bar. In fact, I..."

She trailed off as lesson number one made itself apparent—*Irishmen never sleep.*

Yes, that was definitely poor, exhausted Daniel Flynn strolling down the sidewalk. And as before, he seemed to have attracted a following. The man was definitely smooth.

Frowning, she reassembled her sandwich, focusing on proper alignment of the thick, hearth-baked bread. Maybe she should call to him or somehow acknowledge his presence. She knew it was the polite thing to do. Unfortunately, something about the Irishman left her short-wired on both speech and patience.

"What's wrong with your food?" her sister asked. "You stopped talking to snarl at it."

"It's not the food."

"Then what?"

He neared. Annie needed to do something. Or not. Still ambivalent, she waggled her fingers in a tentative greeting as she decided what to call him. Nothing other than "the Irishman" fit comfortably in her mind.

"Mister Flynn…"

No response from the subject, who was otherwise occupied.

"Uh…Danny…"

Smiling, he chatted with his companions.

"Uh…Dan…uh…" God, she sounded like she'd swallowed the village idiot. She gave one more iteration of his name a try. "Daniel."

Score one for the village idiot. The Irishman was looking her way.

SO ANNIE RUTHERFORD had lost another battle with her conscience, and Daniel's day was to be a casualty. Again. He had seen her, and would have been pleased to keep walking past her crazed brand of moodiness. While he hadn't been quite tired enough to find his carpet appealing, he was too bloody tired to handle bared fangs. Now, though, there was no escape.

"If you don't mind stopping…" he said to his trio of silver-haired new friends. At their cheerful assents, he stepped inside the patio enclosure.

"Hello again, Ms. Rutherford. And just so we get the formalities out of the way, my name's always Daniel, sometimes Dan, but never, on pain of death, Danny."

She frowned at him as if he were a bug ripe for squashing. "We'll compromise. I'll stick with Flynn."

"Ladies," he said after broadening his smile to fend

off her ill-humor, "this is Annie Rutherford, with whom I'll be working. Annie, this is Mrs. Rush, whose father was born in Belfast, and Mrs. Porter, whose grand-daughter is studying in Dublin just now. Beside Mrs. Porter, there, is Mrs. Keane, who's visited my family's pub. They've been showing me around the market. Sharp bargainers, they are, too," he added with a satis-fied nod at the bagfuls of fruits and granolas and what-not he held.

Annie's greeting smile for his companions was warm, genuine and beautiful. In fact, Daniel was very nearly jealous. When she looked back at him, that smile flattened about the edges.

He glanced at her dining partner and raised his brows in enquiry.

"This is my sister, Elizabeth," she said with obvious unwillingness. "Elizabeth, this is Daniel Flynn."

He shifted the packages in his arms and offered her a hand in greeting. "It's grand to meet you."

"Annie was just telling me about you," she said with a calm he found surprising given her volatile sister.

"Then I'll count myself lucky I couldn't hear her."

His comment earned a surprised burst of laughter from Elizabeth. As Daniel took in the siblings, their sim-ilarities became apparent. Elizabeth was a finely pol-ished version of Annie—no freckles, no appealing ripeness to her features. Many, he was sure, would find her the more beautiful of the two sisters. He was find-ing himself of another opinion. At least when Ms. Annie wasn't shooting darts his way.

"Annie says you'll be here until August," Elizabeth prompted.

"It seems a grand place," he said by way of an answer.

"She also said you have no furniture or kitchen supplies."

"True, but how much does a man need?" he teased, giving a nod to his tide-me-over food. "My friends, here, have been taking good care of me."

"Well, how about dinner tomorrow at least?"

"Elizabeth..." Ms. Annie's voice rang a warning note.

Her sister forged on. "We're having an anniversary dinner for our parents at my house. Would you like to join us? I'm sure Annie would have no problem giving you a ride."

Daniel bit back a laugh. He was sure Annie would have a problem, indeed, and in more ways than her sister could imagine. Back home that particular turn of phrase carried a more active—and naked—meaning. But here he was in America, and he'd do well not to grin like a jackass every time someone used it.

"It's a family event. I'd be intruding," he protested.

"No, really you wouldn't. It's going to be a totally mixed bag. You'll enjoy it and fit in perfectly, I promise. Please come."

He should be saying no. In fact, he could see the word shaped on Annie's full lips and telegraphed in her glare. And for that reason and no other, he said, "Thank you, Elizabeth, for the offer. I believe I will."

4

"Unh...ah...ahhhhh!"

"Subtle, guys." Annie knew revenge sex when she heard it. Not once in the time they'd been together had Garth gone for a wild night, a morning quickie, a nooner *and* whatever one called yet another round at nearly five-damn-o'clock on a Sunday evening, up against the living room wall.

Brain fried from endless Internet research, she finished shutting down her computer, pushed away from the desk in the corner of her living room and cranked up the music. An improvement, but it didn't quite cover Garth and Mei. The rhythm was just...off.

The shrill ring of the phone competed against both Coldplay on the radio and her jerkwad neighbors. She cruised back to her desk and picked up the call, harboring the irrational hope that it was the Irishman, canceling.

"Hello?"

No such luck. Elizabeth was on the other end, hot to give one of her "reminder calls."

While her sister provided a run-through of the menu, Annie moved to the kitchen in an effort to escape the Garth 'n Mei show. Phone clamped between her ear and shoulder, she ran cool water into a colander containing the skinny and absurdly expensive beans that Elizabeth had asked her to bring this evening.

"So you needed an Irishman at dinner to be sure you've got the members of the European Union covered, right?" Annie asked in reply to a recitation of the guest list.

Apparently, sarcasm wasn't being served tonight because her sister revved into high gear. "Be charitable. Think of all the people who opened their doors to us when we were traveling with Mom and Dad…all the life-enriching experiences, the wonderful people we've met…"

Annie took the phone away from her ear and held it out, letting Elizabeth's sermonizing embrace the universe. Yeah, so she was endangering her karma by not wanting Daniel Flynn at dinner, but she'd rather gamble with her karma than her sanity.

She brought the phone back within listening distance. Lizzie was still going strong.

"What's going on over there?" her sister demanded. "What's with the music? Are you even listening to me?"

Annie spoke into the mouthpiece of the phone as if it were a microphone, leaving her sister's voice streaming sideways over her shoulder. "Of course I am."

"So what did I tell you to do with the haricots verts?"

Annie sighed. "They're green beans."

"*French* green beans."

"Roger that. *French* green beans."

"It does make a difference, you know."

"Right-o." She would have been more appreciative of the nuances if they were discussing the difference between fake, waxy chocolate and Godiva.

"You're not going to be this moody at dinner, are you?"

"Of course not. Rutherfords are terminally polite."

"Annie…"

Another lecture was simmering, and she had done her best not to swallow the last. She lodged the phone back between ear and shoulder, turned off the water and left the kitchen.

"Look, I'm bringing Flynn and your beans," she said over the music and thumps. "And I'm also trying not to go off on you for inviting him without discussing it with me in the first place."

"I still don't see the problem," her sister said.

"*Really?* How about if that jerk in your office you're always complaining about got to come watch while you had a bikini wax? Or better yet, tag along to the doctor for your annual exam? Just slip your feet in the stirrups, Lizzie… See the problem now?"

"Disgusting, *and* you're overreacting. It's a simple dinner gathering…a little wine, a little conversation. I was hoping you'd be more positive after a night's sleep."

"If I'd had one, maybe." She'd worked late on a task flowchart for the pub launch, then fallen into bed just in time for the first aria from next door. The latest seemed to be reaching its peak.

Annie refused to react, though what she really wished for was a battering ram to punch through the drywall. She turned her back to the banging wall and tried to focus on Elizabeth's cut-back-on-caffeine spiel.

"G-a-a-r-r-r-thhh!"

The only facet of Annie's life that wasn't particularly screwed up was her attitude toward sex…until maybe now. Either Annie was an underachiever or Mei was top of her class. That last howl had to have hit the D above high C. Not that Mei had been carrying a tune…

At least they were finished. Finally. Annie waited a few seconds, inserting uh-huhs as appropriate into Lizzie's speech, then turned the stereo closer to a nonsex-blocking volume.

As she sent a plea for just a few minutes of peace and solitude to the heavens, Annie's front bell sounded. She glanced at her 1960s clock collection on the fireplace mantel. All agreed that she was out of time.

"Flynn's at the door," she said to her sister. "Gotta go."

She rid herself of her lecturing sister, then made her way to her front door. As expected, the Irishman stood on the other side. All in all, it wasn't much of a trade-off.

"Come on in," she said. He wore a dark shirt with light-colored chinos that fit annoyingly well. In one hand he held a bunch of flowers and in the other a paper grocery bag.

Up close he looked more well muscled than she recalled, and not in a vein-popping steroid-case bad way, either. Words began to escape her again, so she focused on the mechanics of getting through the evening.

Once Flynn was inside, she ushered him to the living room and motioned at the couch, which she noticed was stacked with her to-be-read pile of books. "Why don't you move some stuff and have a seat? I'll be ready in just a sec."

For the first time, the Irishman seemed out of place. He waved the bunch of tulips. "It'd be best if I stood."

She paused. "That makes sense. Are those for my sister?"

"No, you, actually. I was hoping to persuade you to call a truce."

The old adage about being wary of Greeks bearing gifts could stretch to one Irishman, as well. Besides, the last time a guy had given her flowers was senior prom, and that had been a nasty-looking glob of dehydrated pink carnations with polyester lace, the presentation of which her boyfriend deludedly thought entitled him to sex in the back of his father's Monte Carlo.

Flynn, however, had no Monte Carlo, so she accepted the flowers. One plump lavender petal quivered beneath her fingertip.

"They're beautiful. Let me find something to put them in."

"And about the truce?"

Annie opened the door to the breakfront that held the vintage china she'd picked up at secondhand shops. In the back rested a sleek Orrefors crystal vase, only slightly chipped on one edge.

"A truce…" She didn't need to be overtly hostile toward him to keep control of this pub death march. In fact, she wasn't exactly sure why she didn't like him. Polite yet distant would do the job. God knew she'd experienced enough of that routine in her life that she should be able to produce a decent facsimile. "I guess I'm game if you are."

"Agreed."

Annie waited for something resembling relief to settle over her, but it wasn't quite there. She remained ticked off at life in general, tired of being ticked off and without the first clue how to change—all of which made her want to explode.

Crystal in one hand and flowers in the other, she closed the china cabinet door with her elbow. Flynn followed her to the kitchen, but lingered in the doorway.

"All those are…?"

She briefly looked over her shoulder to see what he

was looking at. "Salt-and-pepper shakers," she said, giving the array on her counter a distracted glance. Weird, but she seldom noticed them anymore. "I collect them."

"That, I'd figured."

She filled the vase and settled the flowers inside, and Flynn asked about the closest market and other incidentals helpful to a guy in a new place.

Annie answered, but a glut of other words pushed at her chest, making it hurt to breathe. She bagged the beans, snagged her parents' anniversary gift from its perch on her kitchen table and tucked the veggies on top of the basket. The need to let loose grew stronger.

This was like one of those nightmares where she did something freakishly inappropriate, such as dancing naked in the middle of a management meeting. In her dreams she couldn't stop herself from stripping down, and right now she couldn't manage to shut up.

She turned to face Flynn. "I, uh…I…"

His brows rose marginally. "There's something you're wanting to say?"

Such a casual guy. So perfectly collected, while she was a perfect mess. She settled the basket back on the table.

"Okay, I thought I could dodge the big issues for one night, but I've decided it's unhealthy. So here goes…I didn't want you to come to dinner, but not nearly as much as I didn't want you to come to Ann Arbor at all. I know none of this is your fault, but Hal's pub idea came at a rotten time for me, personally, and I really wish the whole mess would disappear. But it's not going to, is it?"

She didn't wait for him to answer. Instead, she got the rest out so maybe she could inhale again. "Tomorrow, when we get to the office, I'll take the lead. When Hal asks questions, I'll answer. I need this first pub together, fast and right. This afternoon, I've been developing a list of potential designers and suppliers. I already have a time line set up and ideas for the chain's theme. While you're here, all you need to do is sit back and relax."

"Theme, you say? You've been busy," he commented in a neutral voice.

"Just doing what I do best."

"And you're telling me to do nothing for the money Hal's paying me?"

"It's not such a bad deal, is it?"

He said nothing, which she could have taken as agreement, except that she didn't quite trust the curve of his mouth. It was too one-sided to be a smile.

"Should I take your silence as a yes?" she asked.

Slowly, the curve stretched its way to the other side of his face. "Do you never relax, Annie Rutherford? It's a Sunday, and I'm about to sit down to dinner with your family and friends. Tomorrow will be here soon enough." He took the gift basket from the table. "Are you ready?"

"I think the question's more whether you're ready to run the gauntlet tonight," she replied as she plucked her purse and keys from the counter.

Flynn laughed. "And here I thought I already had."

Okay, so he had evasion down to an art form. Annie followed him through the living room and to the front door. And as she did, she swore this was the very last time that she'd chase Daniel Flynn's tail.

AS THEY WOVE THEIR WAY through what Annie told him was the University of Michigan's central campus, Daniel attempted to recover from the shock of seeing her home. Was there nothing the woman didn't collect?

He'd been barraged by books, clocks and countless pieces of china in the first room, then stopped dead in the kitchen door.

Daniel had his belongings pared down to the essentials—a filled bookcase in his flat above the pub, his laptop, a fiddle he didn't dare lose—or his mam would kill him—and an old BMW motorcycle under a tarp in a shed behind his brother James's home.

It suffocated him, the thought of all of Annie's things. And made him dread the sight of her sister's house, too. If they possessed some genetic predisposition to clutter, he'd be first at the cocktails and last to finish his after-dinner drink.

Annie pulled into the drive of a three-story house that was a female's fantasy of wood cutwork and folly. Daniel steeled himself—he was clearly fated for a death by claustrophobia. He gathered the two bottles of wine he'd brought—one for Elizabeth and one for the anniversary couple. Perhaps they'd not be missing one if he drank it now.

He looked over at Annie. Frowning, she switched off the car, closed her eyes, then drew a slow breath.

So it wasn't polite to be watching as her breasts rose beneath the skimming fit of her pale blue top. Neither was it customary for him to be so damn interested. Ah, but he was. Subtlety appealed to him in a way that obviousness never would. And Annie Rutherford was subtly delicious right down to her freckles, if also totally mad.

He'd come all this way to do what Hal Donovan had asked, and he'd come as a friend. To give less than his whole effort was an insult, which Ms. Annie should already know. That she'd hold him to a lesser standard than she would herself smacked of insult, too, damn her.

Her eyes opened.

"Ready?" she asked.

Daniel realized he was still staring dead-on at her breasts, no matter where his mind had wandered. And she hadn't mistaken his gaze.

He cleared his throat. "Your parents' names are…?"

"Alison and Max," she replied, eyes narrowed.

"Fine names."

She glared at him for a moment more, clearly debating the merits of an argument over his point of focus. He had to admit to disappointment when she simply said, "Okay. Let's go."

And so they did. They were the first there, and Daniel was vastly relieved to find that the interior of Elizabeth Rutherford's house had far more to do with Asian understatement than with Annie's bric-a-brac. He was left without time to wonder where the Asian aesthetic played in because the sisters did share one trait in common—a love of bossing others about.

Elizabeth put Annie through her paces in the gourmet kitchen. And in what Daniel could only perceive as a case of manure making its way downhill, without so much as a please, Annie ordered him off to the living room to set up the bar. Which was, after all, what he knew best, she'd added.

Her assumption was partially true, at least. He also knew that he gained most in life by watching before speaking and there was a bloody lot to be watching here. Once the bar was set, Daniel poured himself a mineral water, added a couple of ice cubes for company, then settled on a sleek ivory-colored sofa and waited for the show to begin.

He hadn't long to wait, for the Rutherford sisters seemed to have reached a cooking crisis.

"Do the beans still have some snap to them?" he heard Elizabeth ask over the clatter of pots in the kitchen.

"Yes."

"A little or a lot?"

"Hey, it's not like I sit around and quantify the amount of snap in a bean."

Daniel smiled. He could picture the eye roll that had accompanied Annie's words.

"If it's just a little, they'll be limp by the time they're served. They can hold in the warming drawer only so long."

"Wow, Beans 101, courtesy of Ms. Phi Beta Kappa. Why don't you try one for yourself if you don't trust me?"

After a moment's silence he heard a resigned sigh. "They'll have to do."

"You know I don't like to cook, especially for Mom and Dad."

"You need to cut them some slack. They're not as difficult as you make them out to be."

"It kind of depends where you are in the pecking order, doesn't it? I think I'll go make myself a drink."

She was quick on her feet, Ms. Annie. Daniel scarcely had the time to look occupied with the magazine he grabbed from the end table before she appeared.

She gave him a wary hello as she came into the room. "Just getting my mind to a better place," she said as she poured a glass of wine. "Especially since my body's about to sit through another endless discussion of Edo period art."

"Edo?"

"Japanese," she said after a sip. "My mom's an art

historian. Dad's an economist. His specialty's the Pacific Rim. They both teach at U of M."

"Ah," Daniel said for lack of anything better. She was giving the news as if it were bleak, and he had no idea why. He shifted on the sofa, which was a complete triumph of style over comfort.

"Just don't expect any sports chat," she said as she sat opposite him. He hadn't noticed earlier, but she had pretty, slender legs, with a sprinkling of freckles, too.

He looked up to catch her scowling at him. Again.

"You really have to stop doing that."

"Doing what?" he asked, just for the pleasure of increasing her annoyance, which seemed only sporting considering the way she'd worked herself under his skin. He knew what he'd been doing, though it was more involuntary than he cared to admit.

"Stop looking at me."

"You've got a lot of rules," he said, after stringing out the moment with a sip of water.

"What do you mean?"

"Earlier you told me I'm not to think or speak my mind, and now I'm not to look at you. You've taken care of free will, best I can see. Might you have any rules regarding the beat of my heart or how often I'm to breathe?"

She stared into her wineglass. "I— I didn't mean it that way. I'm just setting out the parameters of our relationship."

He allowed himself a smile. "Relationship? Scary word, that."

His comment gained her full attention. Her color rose, as did her voice. "*Work* relationship, okay?"

Just then, the front door chimed.

"Could you get that, Annie?" her sister called from the other room.

She stood and shot him one last frosty gray glare. "We'll finish this later."

"Can't wait," Daniel said, though he dreaded to think how many more rules Annie Rutherford would have manufactured by then.

5

MONDAY DAWNED WITH something damn close to the crow of a cock.

After moaning "Would you shut *up*?" in the general direction of her neighbors, Annie crawled from bed. Four more hours of sleep might have made her passably human, but it wasn't to be. The same stress that had messed with her sleep still rode her hard.

Like it or not, she had to face the indignity that had been last night's dinner. She had to accept that Flynn, with his charm and surprising knowledge of Kyoto—her mother's favorite city—had been the hit of the party. And Annie had been invisible.

Worse than invisible, actually. When Elizabeth tried to turn the conversation to Annie's new assignment, it had become obvious that her parents had only a sketchy concept of what she actually did for a living. She knew they lived in an academic haze, but dammit, that had hurt.

Flynn, of all people, had come to her rescue, distracting everyone with a tale about long-dead royal assassins and the warning issued by the squeaking "nightingale" floor in Kyoto's Imperial Palace.

If she were a good person, she'd probably have felt gratitude. Since all she ended up feeling was grumpy and incredibly low, Annie figured she remained a few reincarnations off from *good*.

She showered, dressed, messed with her makeup and then packed her pub research into her briefcase. By the time she made it to her car, she was as close to running late as she'd ever been.

She was at the corner stop sign waiting for traffic to clear, when in the rearview mirror she saw Flynn strolling down the sidewalk toward her. He stopped at the passenger side, which made her feel duty bound to lower the window.

The Irishman braced his hand on the roof of the car and leaned closer to her. Annie caught the faint scent of cigarettes on him and was unhealthily gleeful at this first sign of human frailty.

"Good morning," he said.

"Good morning," she replied, recalling her vow to be polite yet distant with the guy. "You might as well get in. If you don't, you'll be late."

"Late for what?"

"Work."

"But we're not meeting with Hal till nine."

"So?"

He glanced at the digital clock on her dashboard. "It's not yet eight-twenty."

"You should always be in the office before eight-thirty. Otherwise, you'll make us look bad."

His smile rolled out slow and easy, capturing Annie.

"Ah, so this is another of your rules?" he asked.

"It's not a rule, it's—"

"A parameter."

"Funny." She began to raise her window, hoping to chop off at least one of his fingers.

A car horn sounded from behind them, which distracted her from maiming Flynn. Annie checked her mirror again. It was Mei in her shiny green little Beetle. Garth, too. She couldn't believe that he'd abandoned his eco-friendlier-than-thou standards and gotten into a car. Maybe he'd taken pity on Mei, who couldn't be walking comfortably this morning.

Mei beeped again, impatient chick that she was. Flynn turned and gave a friendly wave.

"So do you want a ride?" Annie fired at him before he decided to bond with the pair.

"A ride?" The Irishman grinned, which, considering her tone of voice, surprised her. "I'm thinking I might."

"Then hurry up and get in."

She moved her briefcase to the back seat, and he climbed in. Once he was buckled, Annie watched for a break in traffic, then zipped out in front of a delivery truck. The truck's driver blasted on his horn, and Flynn braced his hands on the dashboard, muttering something that definitely wasn't in English.

"Sorry, in a hurry," she said to the guy in the truck, not that he could hear. To Flynn she added, "What language was that?"

"Irish. I was saying my last prayers. I've felt safer in a Manhattan cab."

She smiled in spite of herself. "Thanks."

He laughed. "And truly now, thank you for the dinner. It's an interesting group of friends your parents have."

"You're welcome," she said in a tone that she hoped equaled "topic dead."

Flynn took the hint. To fill the silence, Annie fiddled with the radio, searching for a drive-time show that actually played music instead of commercials. When she accepted that she was flat out of luck, she switched it off.

They were nearly to the public parking structure by headquarters when he spoke again. "It was brilliant hearing you speak Japanese last night."

She'd give him points for tenacity. "It's no big deal. I learned out of self-preservation. We lived there for two years."

The warmth of his gaze settled on her long before he spoke. "You undervalue yourself, Annie Rutherford."

Her heart did an odd little flutter.

"I doubt it," she said as she wheeled into a parking spot. By the time she'd turned off the car and pulled the keys from the ignition, Flynn was around to her side of the car, opening the door for her. While she stepped out, he opened the back door and retrieved her briefcase. She took it from him.

As their hands brushed, she felt another small skip of the heart, which left her unthrilled. Since she'd already tanked at the "polite" part of the Flynn control plan, damned if she'd let "distant" die, too.

Over the sound of the car doors closing, Annie heard a greeting coming her way.

"And here I thought chivalry was dead," Sasha called as she came from the line of parked cars opposite them. Once she'd joined them, she checked out Flynn with frank appreciation.

Annie dredged up her last drop of polite. "Daniel Flynn, this is Sasha Donovan. Sasha, Daniel. Your grandfather's hired him to work on the pub launch."

She watched as the two shook hands and exchanged small talk. They looked so right, somehow. Sasha, with her willowy shape and dramatic features, was the kind of woman made for a guy like Flynn. They'd marry, be superbreeders and have yet another generation of mind-blowingly gorgeous humans who made Annie's sort feel as though they were a less-evolved species. She wasn't so much jealous as resigned.

They made their way out of the parking structure and turned left, toward Main Street.

"That's headquarters," Annie said, pointing at the building for Flynn's benefit.

Flynn cupped his hand above his eyes, shielding his gaze from the morning sun. "It looked bigger on the Internet."

"Trust me, lots of things do," Sasha joked.

Flynn chuckled. "I'll not be touching that comment."

Sasha and sexual banter went hand in hand, but this time it wasn't sitting well with Annie. She gripped tighter to her briefcase.

"Did Hal get you set up with human resources?" she asked Flynn. The words came out sharper than she'd intended.

Sasha gave her a what's-up-with-you? look.

Eternally unruffled Flynn replied, "I'm to go up and see Mrs. D'Onfrio."

"Okay."

They entered Donovan's lobby, with its wall-engulfing artsy mural of Hal and his four surviving sons looking down on their pizza kingdom. While Sasha and the Irishman continued to chat, Annie impatiently waited for the elevator. It arrived, and she pushed the top floor button for Flynn and the less prestigious seventh floor for Sasha and herself.

"You'll find Mrs. D. straight ahead when you get to your floor," Annie told Flynn.

He nodded. "I'll be seeing you at nine, then?"

"Yes." The elevator bumped to a stop.

As the door slid open, Flynn said, "It was grand to meet you, Sasha. And Annie…" His voice grew low and intimate. "Be thinking of what you're worth today."

"Okay," she said, not sure how else to answer. Annie hurried out of the elevator and joined Sasha just before the door closed.

Sasha hauled Annie into her office, then quickly closed the door. She leaned against it as though weak-kneed, then practically purred, "Where'd my grandfather find *him?*"

"A souvenir from his vacation," Annie said while dumping her briefcase onto a guest chair.

"I shop at all the wrong places," Sasha said, abandoning her take-me pose. "So is he why you didn't call me back this weekend? I'd have kept him all to myself, too."

Annie was about to offer up a flip "Want him?" but the words lodged somewhere midwindpipe. This was bad. Very bad.

"He's incredible," Sasha enthused.

Annie briefly rested her hand against her throat. Beneath her fingertips, her pulse ran rabbit-scared. She gave a casual smile, then walked to the window. On the sidewalk below, a lazy summertime flow of morning coffee-and-newspaper seekers strolled past.

"Come on, Annie, admit that he's hot," her friend said.

"He's also baggage we don't need," she replied, hoping a tacit admission would shut Sasha up. "Some years behind a bar and the ability to talk to anybody, anywhere about nearly anything are his only qualifications. He's like a walking invitation for people to get off task." Herself included.

"You know, it's a good thing I love you because you can be such a snob," Sasha said.

A tightness in her voice drew Annie's gaze from the streetscape.

"Sometimes I don't think you have any idea how lucky you are," her friend continued. "Not everyone plans ten years in advance and takes the right step every time, Annie. Some of us are more fallible, okay? So what if he doesn't have your kind of pedigree? Do you know what it feels like to only be trusted with stuff like which kids' soccer teams we're going to sponsor? Or how many pizzas we need to send over to the charity skate-a-thon? Or, 'Sasha, what shade of ivory should we use on the cocktail party invitations?'"

Annie drew in a breath. "Sasha—"

She turned away. "Shit. I'll catch you later, okay?"

Sasha was out the door before Annie could even begin to absorb what had just happened. She walked to her desk, sat down and absently traced her finger over the gold embossed initials on the crimson leather portfolio her brother had sent her when she'd finished grad school.

Annie had known Sasha since tenth grade. Annie's parents had been offered jobs at the university, and she'd been dumped into yet another new school. Some people made friends quickly, but she'd never been one of them. Annie had tried her hardest to act as though she didn't give a rat's ass that she had no one to sit with at lunch or hang out with after school. Then quirky, bohemian Sasha had marched into the middle of her life.

Through the years when Annie had stayed in Ann Arbor for undergrad, then made the hour-long commute to Michigan State for her MBA, Sasha had flitted from major to major, city to city, never quite finishing college. It hadn't seemed a big deal. Her employment had always been Donovan guaranteed. She'd always seemed content, too. Who wouldn't be, born into a pizza empire?

Annie pushed away from her desk, grabbed her coffee mug and wandered down to the galley tucked between two conference rooms. She eyed the bag of bagels someone had brought in for mass consumption, but found her stomach oddly hollow, and passed them by. She filled her coffee mug and returned to her office, keeping her eyes low. She wasn't in the mood to manufacture Irish-pub enthusiasm for well-wishers, ill-wishers or the flat-out nosey.

Door closed, she called Sasha, got her voice mail and left an are-you-okay? message. Sasha didn't call back, so Annie leafed through her presentation materials for Hal until just before nine o'clock. At least this meeting was one thing she could get right. Annie triple-checked her file, then went upstairs.

"They're waiting for you," Mrs. D'Onfrio said as she approached. "Go on in."

After a quick knock, Annie opened the double doors to Hal's office. He wasn't behind his desk. Instead, he and Flynn were in the more informal seating area, deep in conversation. Annie had to say that they looked pretty cozy.

Hal glanced at his watch. "Nine o'clock already? Come on over, Annie, and have a seat."

Since Hal was in the only chair, she was stuck joining Flynn on the horses-and-hounds-print couch. She did, settling into a spot at least a foot farther away from him than office protocol required. She set her research folder on the low table in front of them and pulled out the CD she'd burned yesterday afternoon.

"I have a short presentation ready," she said, gesturing at the computer and small projection screen on the opposite wall. "Should I set it up?"

"Not just yet," Hal said, with a casual wave of his hand. "Daniel was just telling me that you had him to a family dinner last night, Annie. Maybe one day he can return the favor. You'd like Ireland."

Only if she could travel by ship.

Flynn's mouth developed that unsettling semismile. She needed to get this morning back on track.

"So," she said to Hal, "if you're not in the mood for a full presentation, how about a quick run-through of what I've done?" She didn't wait for an answer, since odds were it wouldn't be to her liking anyway. "I've already found one company that specializes in pub designs and an architectural salvage warehouse just over in Ypsilanti that should be able to locate vintage materials for us."

She reached into her document file and began spreading pages across the cocktail table. "Of course, I'm still tracking down the best menu consultant to bring on the team. There's a former executive chef from—"

"Rein it in, Annie," Hal said. "That's all good, but you're ahead of yourself."

She froze, one hand halfway in the file. Hal usually liked the way she surfed the front edge of a project. "In what way?"

"Before we discuss any of this, you'll be going to Chicago, then Seattle. Plan on being away for a minimum of three days."

"Seattle, as in Washington?" she heard herself ask.

"I think that would be the one," Flynn replied. Hal laughed, and Annie felt seriously outnumbered.

"We'd fly there?" she asked, both knowing and dreading the answer. For the past several years of her employment, she'd been able to duck any mention of her little problem with airplanes. It wasn't so much that she refused to get on one. It was more like she'd expend every last brain cell trying to find a way to avoid it.

"Flying beats walking," Hal replied.

She glanced at Flynn, who was wearing a sympathetic look. It rattled her to think he could be intuitive enough to understand that she hated air travel. Sometimes it seemed that in the Donovan corporate culture, a tattoo reading *planes suck* emblazoned across her forehead would go unnoticed. In this instance, at least, she much preferred flying below the radar. Or not at all.

"I don't...I..." Aligning the papers on the table, she drew a breath and tried again. "I don't have time to go to Seattle. I suppose if I really had to, I could drive to Chicago. I mean, it's only a few hours." God, the village idiot had returned, in full babble mode. "Or Flynn could go and send back a report."

"If I wanted Daniel to go alone, that's who I'd be sending. Do you have a problem with this, Annie?"

She had a great many, but she'd yank her liver through her nose before she'd bare yet another weakness.

"No problem, just time-management issues," she said. "It makes no sense to send both of us."

Hal's brows drew together, two shaggy silver caterpillars battling. "Ninety percent of what will make this first pub a success is atmosphere. Daniel says that Chicago and Seattle have two of the most vibrant pub communities in the States, plus they're the spots where he knows the most staff to raid. I want both of you to take in the sounds, taste the food, listen to the music. And most of all, Annie, I want you to use that intuition of yours and tell me what else it is the customers want."

"Why don't we commission a market study?" Like any nonnutcase businessman would do, she wanted to add. Except Annie knew that when it came to this project, he'd chucked sane right out the window.

"I want more than someone else's data. I want your impressions and whatever staff Daniel can recruit."

She turned to Flynn, who had apparently forgotten great chunks of her take-a-back seat talk. "Fast work."

"Just doing what I do best," he said.

She was being served up her own words, and they tasted rotten.

"No fussing, Annie," Hal said. "This will be an easy trip. Mrs. D'Onfrio will make the arrangements, and all you need to do is show up." He looked at Daniel. "Will tomorrow be too early for you?"

"Not a bit. I doubt they'll be delivering my furniture so soon, even if I choose it today."

Did no one think she had a life?

"I need a few days, Hal," she said. "Thursday would be better."

Her boss shook his head. "No, tomorrow. We're on a deadline, and we both know you don't have any personal engagements keeping you here. No one who works around-the-clock could."

She had seen him pull the autocratic act on his sons in management meetings countless times before. When they'd been in the line of fire, it had seemed funny. Now that it was aimed at Annie, she was nearly nostalgic for last night's brand of family mortification. She turned her head just enough to cut Flynn from her peripheral vision. One more pitying look would send her straight to the vending machine with a roll of quarters.

"My personal life is just that," she said as crisply as she could.

"You go tomorrow. If you have a dog or something, make my granddaughter feed it."

Annie rose, then picked up the folder filled with a wasted weekend's work. "Your granddaughter's name is Sasha," she said, just ticked enough to venture into rocky Donovan relationships. "And I don't have a dog."

Though she'd trade her MBA for a leash and muzzle on Hal Donovan.

6

DANIEL WATCHED AS Annie lifted her obese carry-on above her head and tried to lodge it into the bin. Not even taking into account the house-on-wheels she'd checked, she'd packed far too much. She teetered backward, endangering the souls across the aisle. He lifted the bag from her hands.

"I've got it," he said, then hefted it into place and latched the compartment. "You've the window seat…just go on in."

"Okay," she said, but still lingered. A worry line seemed to have taken up residence between her brows, and her gray eyes lacked their usual spark. After watching her talk her way around her fear in Hal's office, Daniel was sure that even boarding the plane had been a struggle for Annie. Still, though, here they were and damned if he'd let her back out now.

"Annie, you're holding up matters." He gave a "sorry" to the people waiting behind them. "Would you rather have my aisle seat?"

"Yes."

She moved just enough to let him edge past. Daniel considered the brush of his body against hers a reward, brief though it was. He knew he'd just consigned himself to having his knees to his chin all the way to O'Hare, but the cause was noble—getting this plane from the tarmac without Annie Rutherford being tarred and feathered. After nearly smacking his head on the overhead bin, he folded into his seat.

"Wait!" she blurted. "I've changed my mind. I want the window."

"Come on, already," someone groused.

"Sit and we'll switch when everyone is by," he said. She didn't move.

He motioned to the empty seat between them. "Just set your briefcase there." He felt as though he were talking her back from a ledge.

"But—"

"Annie…"

"Okay."

Passengers pushed their way by as soon as she was in her seat.

"Nervous flyer," Daniel said to the worst of the glares and eye rolls.

Once the aisle was again clear, Annie stood. "Time to trade."

"You're sure of this?" he asked. "It's not some trick to make me hit my thick skull while getting out, is it?"

She nearly smiled. "I'd like to be able to look out the window."

And as he'd like to be able to occasionally stretch his legs, the deal was made.

Daniel resettled in the aisle seat, buckled his seat belt and closed his eyes. He could hear Annie next to him, apparently wrestling with her briefcase.

"You'll have to put that under the seat in front of you, ma'am," a flight attendant said.

"Okay, just a sec." More scrabbling about from Ms.

Annie, then finally silence. Daniel let tension ease away, leaving him lax.

Usually, while sitting on a flight, he'd dream. He would block the noise of the other passengers, focusing instead on whatever bit of fiction he happened to be working on. He'd put nothing on paper, just let the ideas simmer warm and slow the way his mam did with her best lamb stew. Then as soon as he was back on the ground, he'd write his tale like a man possessed.

Click-click…click-click

A sound—and not at all a pleasant one—crept into his consciousness. He kept his eyes closed, willing himself to that still place…that quiet place…

Click-click…click-click

Feck it all.

Click-click…click-click

It was Annie, he knew it. He opened one eye just far enough to see what the woman was doing. She had a leather-bound notebook open in her lap and a retractable ballpoint pen in her left hand.

Click-click…click-click

She stared straight ahead, her thumb working the little button atop the pen. He settled his hand over hers.

She yelped.

He briefly squeezed her hand tighter and said, "If you don't mind stopping the business with the pen?"

She tugged her hand from beneath his. "Sorry."

"No problem," he said, then let his eyes close again. *Click-click.*

"Sorry," he heard her say again. "Nervous habit."

Giving up his Zen state for lost, Daniel focused on Annie as she slid the pen back into its loop on the inside of the portfolio.

She had perfectly polished oval nails, petal-pink and enough to make him wish he could nibble on them, if she'd not take him as a fetishist—which she would.

The flight attendant began her recitation of the safety information. Annie listened avidly, which was exactly what he'd expect from her. When the plane taxied, she squeezed her eyes shut and gripped the armrests so tightly that her knuckles shone white.

Again he wrapped his fingers over hers. Annie's eyes flew open. She looked at their hands—one covering the other—and a pink nearly matching her nails began to color her cheeks.

Daniel waited for her to grow all prickly and pull her hand away. She didn't, though. She relaxed and accepted the comfort he offered. The plane took to the air and soon finished the last bumps and jolts that had a way of making one a believer in a higher authority.

"Do you have to be so nice?" she asked once all was settled.

He smiled at this patent bit of Annie-ness. "Sorry. It's hereditary."

It was more than that, though. God help him, he wanted her to like him, and not simply because they'd be together for the coming weeks. He wanted her to laugh when he teased her, to listen when he offered ideas. And he wasn't exactly opposed to finding out if she had any places the sun hadn't kissed with a scattering of freckles.

After slipping her hand away, she relaxed against her seat and closed her eyes. Smiling, he did the same. Try as he might, though, his manuscript—now damn near overdue to his editor—wouldn't fill his mind. It was far more taken by imaginings of sleek white skin sprinkled with gold. Before long, the plane was descending. Daniel went to reach for Annie's hand again.

"I'm okay. Really," she said.

It was grand that one of them was, since the smile she gave him was nearly sufficient to stop his heart. Once they landed, he averted any further in-aisle crises by retrieving her monstrous carry-on and wrestling it off the plane for her.

"I can handle it," she said, trying to tug the bag from him as they joined the sea of people in the terminal.

"I've no doubt of that," he replied, but kept it just the same.

They made their way to the baggage-claim area. In time his suitcase made its way around the carousel. He grabbed it and waited for Annie's beast, which seemed to have opted for a late, grand entrance.

Or perhaps it wasn't arriving at all. Annie walked to the mouth of the carousel and tried to peer into the opening. As she leaned forward, Daniel half feared that she planned to crawl against the flow and visit the baggage handlers.

She returned to him. "This doesn't look good. All my clothes are in that bag."

He chose diplomatic silence, which proved to be of little comfort. A few lonely bags soon circled around and around.

Annie began to pace. "See? This is why I hate traveling. Just once, I'd like to go someplace and have my luggage arrive with me."

"Come on," he said, lifting his bag. She glared at it, as though it were responsible for hers having gone missing. He approached a group of uniformed workers.

"Is that the last of the bags from flight 586?"

"Afraid so."

Annie stepped forward. "Well, you're one piece short."

The man who'd spoken hooked a thumb in the direction of the far wall. "That door."

"Great," she muttered.

Once in front of the claims counter, Daniel did his best to offer moral support. Annie gave the agent her particulars and then matched her missing bag to a photo on a large plastic card with generic suitcase mug shots.

"It's close to that one," she said.

Had Daniel been inclined to sacrifice Annie's good graces for honesty, he'd have told the man that it was "close" only if the chosen bag was first force-fed for weeks on end.

When Annie had her lost bag receipt, he tried to move her along toward the cab line.

"Give me a second to get my act together," she said, then sat on a bench near the exit, dropping her carry-on next to her.

Optimistic that this would be a short pick-me-up, Daniel remained standing.

"You'll be fine, you know," he said. "Your suitcase might well beat us to the hotel."

"Or not. And we're supposed to leave for Seattle Thursday morning. What if it doesn't catch up to us by then?"

He scrambled for a positive spin on the situation.

Shopping! Most women he knew loved to shop, and he doubted that Annie was an exception, given the clutter in her home.

"We've nothing to do until night, and Eva told me that our hotel's close to shopping. You could always pick up some clothes to tide you over."

"I hate buying clothes. It's too depressing." She frowned. "Who's Eva?"

"Hal's secretary...Mrs. D'Onfrio."

"Mrs. D.'s first name is Eva?"

The question—and especially Annie's shocked tone—confused him. He was sure she'd been working at Donovan Enterprises for years. "Didn't you know that?"

She didn't answer. Instead, she dug through her bag, heavy with everything but clothes, and extracted a box of tissues. Daniel was going to ask if no travel-size version had been available, but quickly realized she'd planned well.

He'd seen her take the distracted disregard of her parents with not much more than a raising of the brows.

He'd silently applauded as she'd given gruff Hal Donovan as good as she'd been handed.

But Annie Rutherford had just reached her limit and started to cry. And she was doing it with flair.

ANNIE HAD NO CLOTHES, her best friend refused to speak to her and now Daniel Flynn knew Mrs. D'Onfrio's first name.

Maybe the name thing was no big deal, but on top of the lost suitcase and Sasha's constant call screening, it sure felt like one. Hot tears streaked down her face, probably running her nonwaterproof mascara onto her neck. Sobs collected in her throat until they escaped in one long, jittery gasp.

Annie wasn't a woman who could cry prettily, and she had zero tolerance for anyone who could. But, up until this moment, she'd always been able to hold off meltdowns until she was alone. She held a crumpled tissue up to her face, but it wasn't enough to hide her.

One after another, she pulled two more from the box on her lap.

"Annie?"

She looked up. Weight balanced on bent legs and the balls of his feet, Flynn was nearly eye-to-eye. If she weren't so totally off the deep end, she might have gotten a grin out of the alarmed look on his face. It was a sure bet that not many women had come unglued in front of his perfection.

"I'm sorry," she managed to say past the tears. "This is so stupid." She blew her nose, then wiped her eyes. "I can't believe I'm…I'm…" Saying the word aloud would make her feel like an even bigger weenie, so she busied herself pulling another tissue from the box.

"Can I get you some water, or…" He looked around, then back at her. "Or what would you like?"

He was so nice that it was becoming impossible to dislike him.

She hazarded a glance at the area. At least nobody other than the Irishman seemed to be watching her. After all, what was one snot-filled female in the big scheme of things?

Comforted by her total and customary anonymity, Annie began to wad up the tissues on her knees. With those in one hand, she used her other to jam the tissue box back into her carry-on.

She stood. "I think I'd just like to get out of here."

Flynn had her bag over his shoulder almost as quickly as she'd spoken the words. Soon they were settled in a cab and he was saying, "The Almont Hotel, please."

During the drive into the city, he seemed to sense that she needed silence. Or maybe he was quiet for fear of setting off another crying jag. Either way, Annie simply looked at the cars, the highway overpasses and finally downtown Chicago, once it came into view.

Soon they pulled up to the canopied entrance of their hotel. The Almont was an older place, not five-star imposing, but definitely posh. A bellman gathered their bags from the cab's trunk. Or at least what bags Annie still had to her name.

She and Flynn made their way through the revolving door and into a large lobby with maroon carpet underfoot and a crystal chandelier overhead. Annie registered for them, handed the bellman their room keys and followed as he led them to the elevator.

She was still fairly numb from the whole airport experience, so it wasn't until they were heading swiftly upward that she realized Flynn was in the room next to hers. The thought somehow pleased her, a definite sign that she was going soft where he was concerned.

"I've some friends I need to catch up with," he said as they trailed down the hallway after the bellman. "But after that, I was thinking maybe nine o'clock in the lobby is a good time for us to meet."

Annie checked her watch. It wasn't yet four o'clock, Michigan time, and she had a long night ahead. At least with the bonus of an hour's time difference between Ann Arbor and Chicago, she could easily fit in a nap, shower and meal. Otherwise, she'd be a zombie by midnight and totally worthless by last call.

"Nine works for me," she said to Flynn.

"Ma'am," the bellman said, opening her door with a flourish.

Annie walked in and smiled. The sole upside that she could see to traveling was the chance to stay in a place like this. Unable to help herself, she hurried to the window and took in the view. It wasn't Manhattan, but damn, it was close.

Realizing that Flynn still had to get to his room, she tipped the bellman and thanked him. In a matter of moments, she could catch the faint sounds of the Irishman settling in.

Annie snooped in the honor bar, coveting the big-bucks-a-bite chocolate. She checked out the toiletries lined up on the bathroom counter, inventorying what would be going on to Seattle with her. Finally, she dug into her carry-on.

At least she'd done one smart thing and packed an extra pair of underwear in the bag. She tucked the silky blue bit into an otherwise empty drawer. The sight brought home just how alone she was.

Annie picked through her bag until she found her travel candle. She removed the tin's top and set the candle on the cocktail table in front of the loveseat. After a brief search for matches, the calming scent of lavender filled the air.

"Almost like home," she said in a lame attempt to convince herself. But if she were home, she could change out of her wrinkled khakis and into something clean for the night. And Sasha would be going with her. Or not.

Refusing to get sucked into another pityfest, Annie walked back to the window and looked to her right. According to the cabbie—and apparently Mrs. D.—Michigan Avenue was just up at the corner. And on that stretch of broad road were countless stores calling out for her credit card.

True, she hated picking through racks of stuff designed for skinny size twos, hated that most clothes sagged on her waist and seized her butt in a death grip. But at this moment, her hatred for feeling grungy and gritty outweighed even that. Before she could chicken out, she blew out the candle, pulled her purse from her carry-on and left the room. After a stop at the bell captain's stand to ask that her missing suitcase—should it magically arrive—be brought straight to her room, Annie was off.

Maybe it was a positive flow of the cosmos's energy returning to her life, or some other such crapola. Or maybe it was the fact that she was too desperate to be picky, but Annie found new clothes—lots of them.

All those how-to-dress shows playing on the television while she'd worked at home late into the night seemed to have had a subliminal effect. She'd never really listened, yet their advice had sunk in. Annie carried bagfuls of "dramatic" necklines, "concealing" wide-legged pants and "nonclingy" skirts. Nobody would be following her sorry ass down the street, conducting a secret filming of her fashion disasters.

Back in her room, she was bummed to see that this new positive flow hadn't carried her missing bag back to her, but that would have been expecting too much of the cosmos. Annie spread her purchases across the bed, feeling a thrill of excitement over each of them. She wondered if Flynn would notice the difference, then wondered why she was wondering. Before she got too confused, she went to take a shower.

It was nearly seven o'clock when she finished blow-drying her hair and anchored the dryer back into the wall. The click of it locking into place was followed by a thump from outside the bathroom. Annie peeked out to confirm that she was still alone, though odds were good that no one had broken through the security lock or scaled the outside of the building to the fifteenth floor.

Yup, she was alone, though another thump sounded from an adjoining room. Annie shrugged. Such was life in a hotel—not to mention her own home. Standing in front of the mirror, she dabbed her pulse points with the perfume sample she'd picked up while shopping. More muffled thumps—thumps of a certain rhythm—distracted her. It was almost as though Garth 'n Mei had taken their show on the road.

"No way," she muttered. She walked back into the bedroom, grabbed the television remote from the nightstand and pushed the on button.

Out of reflex, Annie glanced up at the television to check out the channel. At that moment—facing the wall between herself and the noise—she made the connection. Flynn was in that room. She sat down hard on the edge of the bed. Maybe she wasn't hearing what she thought she was. He could be exercising. Or moving furniture.

Quiet fell next door. Annie spent a dozen heartbeats waiting for the next shoe—or whatever—to drop, but silence reigned. She shook off her case of the creeps and began to dress, half listening to the steady talk of the all-news network.

As she readied, she convinced herself that she'd jumped to conclusions. Garth and Mei's sexual marathon had messed with her mind. She was like one of Pavlov's dogs, except she was conditioned to believe that thumps—no matter how innocuous—equaled sex. Nothing was going on next door.

Still, the thought of Flynn naked—though far preferably with her—was a tough one to lose. She'd never fantasized much about the guys she worked with. Then again, no one as hot as Daniel Flynn had ever been in Donovan's headquarters. If the warm shiver dancing through her right now was any indicator, she had a feeling that over the next few months her fantasy life was going to be rich.

"Spank me!" a female voice cried suddenly from next door. "Do it!"

Annie froze, flirty black skirt halfway zipped. Kind of hot and squirmy iced down to grossed out.

"Harder!"

Annie finished dressing as though the fire alarm had just sounded. She swept her makeup off the counter and into her new bag, then added the items she'd need for the night—digital camera, notepad, credit card and room key.

Now if she only had some pepper spray.

7

ANNIE RUTHERFORD wasn't always a woman of her word.

This revelation was nothing short of a gobsmack to Daniel, who'd watched for her in the hotel lobby until nearly nine-forty. Being Irish, he held a loose appreciation of time and was willing to wait. Not to mention that the chance to go outside and sneak a cigarette—truly his last—had also held some appeal. Still, even an Irishman knew when casual crossed the line to late. After a call to Annie's room had gone unanswered, he'd ventured to the bar, where he'd found her.

She'd looked at him over the rim of her martini and informed him that she'd be ready to "get this over with" once she'd finished her dinner. That meal had consisted of French fries, shrimp cocktail and chocolate cake. At least she was open to diversity.

"We'll be starting at Mulvaney's," he told her as they finally stepped outside the hotel.

"A chain with locations in L.A., Vail, Chicago, Coconut Grove and Boston," she shot back, eyes straight ahead. "A moderately successful IPO two years ago. Gross annual sales in excess of thirteen million."

So they were back to the sharp-tongued Ms. Annie who'd met him at the airport days earlier. "Grand then, you've heard of it."

She turned left and marched down the walk. "I did my research."

He moved a step ahead of her. "Then you'd be knowing you're headed the wrong way?"

That, at least, brought her up short.

"No sense of direction," she replied before turning about.

As they traveled the blocks to the pub, Daniel tried some chat, but she limited her responses to two words or less. And not bloody once would she look his way.

"Is something wrong?" he asked as they walked past the bright shop windows on Michigan Avenue.

"No," she said in a cheery voice that somehow also carried a layer of frost. Where did women learn how to do that? It had to be some sort of skill passed from mother to daughter in utero.

Daniel stretched out his stride. He'd never had difficulty keeping up with a woman half his damn size. "Did I miss a message? Was I to meet you in the bar?"

"No message."

Other than the one she was sending now. He considered himself a fair sort of man. He didn't mind taking a kick in the arse when he'd done wrong. Problem of it was, he'd done nothing wrong.

"Turn here," he said when they reached Ontario Street.

She nodded.

And he got not another word out of her the rest of the way to Mulvaney's. He opened the pub's door, shaking his head at the layers of paint some poor fool had had to coat the bloody thing with to make it look old. Next he'd be finding water stains artfully applied to the ceiling.

He glanced back and discovered that Her Royal Highness wasn't ready to enter.

"Not yet," she said while pulling out a camera.

Daniel ushered in two women who'd been walking behind them. "But it's dark," he said to Annie.

"I'll use a flash."

He stepped away from the door and patiently waited while she took photos of the pub's sign, trim and whatnot. Finally, she tucked the camera back into her handbag.

"Shall we?" he asked, gesturing at the entrance.

"Fine."

Right, then. About as fine as a three-bottle whiskey hangover. Still, Daniel knew no way through this evening but to finish it.

He was holding the door open for her when she said, "Hang on."

He waved on two more couples and wondered whether his friend Brian might be seeking a doorman for the place. He was well auditioned by now.

Annie beckoned him over, then headed around the corner. Against his better judgment, Daniel followed. She stopped in front of what had to be the dozenth cell phone store he'd seen that day. The glow from the street lights gave him the unhappy set of her face. She wasn't alone in that.

"I think we need to have a talk," she said.

And here he'd been fairly certain that she'd forgotten how.

Daniel watched as she gripped the straps of the handbag she'd slung over her shoulder. His gaze traveled downward—Ms. Annie had been shopping. If he weren't so balls-out irked at the way she was acting, he might tell her that she looked utterly sexy. Her fitted white top and short black print skirt celebrated a figure made to know the sweep of a man's hands. His, perhaps.

"I'm a pretty liberal person," she announced. "You can't live in a college town without having seen—or heard—nearly everything once."

Daniel was sure this was leading somewhere, but just now he was as directionless as Annie.

"And I don't believe in prying into people's personal lives. I mean, different strokes for different folks and all that. But here's the thing, Flynn. You and I have to work together. I can be as professional as the next person, but I don't think I can sit through meetings and whatever without thinking about…about…"

She'd stretched out that last word until he felt as though he were sitting for a fill-in-the-blank exam. "About what?"

"You know what!"

He shook his head. "I wouldn't be asking if I did."

"I *heard* you, Flynn…in your *room.*"

He was beginning to believe that he was nearly as thick as his eejit brothers. "My room? The hotel room?"

She stared intently at the concrete beneath their feet. "Yes."

"The room next to yours?"

"Yes, the room next to mine. Are you going to make me spell this out?"

He'd begun to grasp the general idea, but remained tempted to ask for specifics simply for entertainment's sake. But he also recalled her tears at O'Hare, and he never wanted to make her cry.

"Annie, I changed rooms this afternoon," he said. "The cold water tap in mine wasn't closing well. I went to tell you, but you weren't there." He shrugged. "It didn't seem worth leaving a message when I knew I'd be seeing you tonight."

Finally, she met his eyes. "This afternoon? Not tonight?"

"Not long after we'd checked in," he confirmed.

"But I heard…"

"It wasn't me, though I can be guessing what you heard."

Her laughter was muffled, but there nonetheless. "You might be in the ballpark, but trust me, you can't guess."

He wasn't sure whether to be pleased or insulted that she'd imagined him engaging in obviously other than the standard activities, and so soon after they'd arrived, too. No decision on the point seemed to best suit the bill. Nor did he have to talk, because Annie was now deep in discussion with herself.

"Wow," she said as she paced three strides away. "You weren't even in there." She tipped back her head and laughed. "Embarrassing. Major-league embarrassing." Hands on hips, she looked at the night sky for a moment, then walked the three steps back to him.

"I take it you won't be giving me the gritty details of what you heard?"

"No time soon," she said, softening the words with a smile. "But I do owe you an apology. Even if it had been you in that room, really, it's none of my business." She paused for a moment, frowning. "You know, maybe it's the stress of traveling. I'm not very good at it."

"You're doing a grand job," Daniel said, feeling charitable. Ms. Annie had apologized, and even to his skeptical ears it had sounded real.

He tried to imagine how he'd feel had he heard Annie

making love. The first word that came to him was no surprise—excited. Hard. One after another, the thoughts rolled.

Hungry.

Angry.

Jealous.

Damn, he hadn't known her a week and he was acting as though she were his!

Daniel took a mental step back and tried to grab hold of his common sense. Perhaps it wasn't so much Annie who appealed, as it was the challenge she represented. He'd been seized by the goal of swaying a woman who could scarcely stand to look at him. Except he knew that wasn't the full truth. If she hated him, she'd not care if he had women three-deep lining the hotel's hallways.

Then what was it about Annie? It occurred to him that for all the girlfriends he'd had, he really didn't know feck-all about attraction. Just as quickly, he accepted that he was better off that way, too. He'd rather go with the moment than think it to bloody death.

"So is my apology accepted?" she asked.

"It is." He took Annie's hand and drew her back around the corner. "And now it's time to have some fun."

Which was, he had begun to suspect, something that Annie Rutherford sorely needed.

ANNIE HAD NEVER BEEN in anything resembling a real pub. As she looked around Mulvaney's, with its expensive furnishings and fixtures, she suspected that her record still held. This was a pub on steroids, one whose owner had the cash for the best of everything. She knew she should be puzzling out why Flynn had chosen to bring her here in search of authenticity, but she was too giddy with relief to go beneath the surface.

Thank God it hadn't been Flynn on the receiving end of that "spank me!" command. She'd just begun to like him, to believe that he was possibly more than the sum of his good looks and glib tongue.

"Let me give word we're here," Daniel said, edging with her to one of the few open spots in the busy pub.

Annie surveyed the place, then snapped a few more pictures. She'd bet that the tables were wait-listed for a good hour or more. It didn't look as though the people waiting especially minded—always a good sign. In the very front of the pub, a group of people sat on a combination of benches, bar stools and chairs in a circle. They were drinking and talking at the moment, but all had an instrument of one sort or another at rest.

She glanced over at Flynn, who was smiling and laughing with the hostess.

"Come on back to the service bar," he said once the conversation was finished. "There's someone I want you to meet."

The floor was noisy and crowded, but Flynn took her hand and ran interference for them, weaving through groups with such confidence that Annie felt as though she was witnessing the pub version of the parting of the Red Sea.

At the far end of the long mahogany-colored bar was a small annex that she knew was used to tend to servers' orders. On the edge of this area, Flynn stopped in front of a man wearing an emerald-green polo shirt with the Mulvaney's logo. He was shorter than Flynn and had red hair that had begun to recede. He and Flynn engaged in that handshake/backslap ritual that was exclusively a male greeting. When they were done, both turned to her.

"Annie," Flynn said over the noise, "this is Brian Naughton, an old friend from university. Brian's in charge of everything east of the Mississippi, unless he's been overstating his importance."

"Only the Mulvaney's Pubs," Brian qualified. "Welcome, Annie. Any friend of Daniel's is a woman to be pitied."

Flynn laughed. "Save the insults. Annie has a low enough opinion of me already."

Annie shook hands with Brian. "It's nice to meet you."

"And you," Flynn's friend said. "Daniel's said he's going to be working with you for a while."

"He's helping get a project off the ground."

Brian nodded. "So he's mentioned. Can I get you something to drink?"

She'd learned on Friday night that alcohol and emotion were a toxic mix in her system. "Just some water, thanks."

"Daniel?"

He eyed the bar. "A pint of stout, I'm thinking."

"Maura, water and a pint," Brian called to the service bartender.

The water appeared almost instantaneously. The pint, Annie noted, was a slower process, with the glass three-quarters poured, then left to settle.

Annie thanked Brian for the water and sipped at it while the two guys caught up on common friends.

"So, Annie, have you been with the Donovan family long?" Brian asked as he handed Flynn his now fully poured pint.

"A little over five years," she answered, scooting

back a bit to let a waiter by, his tray heavy with drinks. She bumped into Flynn, who settled a calming hand on her shoulder. At least it should have been calming, except for the jump to her pulse.

"Ah, that's nothing, yet," Brian said. "I'm nearing ten years with Mulvaney's."

"Either sounds like torture to me," Flynn commented.

"And sometimes to me," Brian replied, then raised a cautionary hand. "Don't be getting me wrong, I have the perfect job for my particular talents." He smiled at Annie, then added, "Daniel, here, has this way of making the rest of us poor work-a-day slobs wonder 'what if?' We don't travel half the year and we never meet royalty."

"Royalty? At your family pub?" she asked Flynn.

"No, unless you count Mad Johnny McMahon, the self-proclaimed King of Clifden. The royalty—and minor at that—was actually an interview for a magazine I write for. You won't find it outside Europe."

"Ah. Small potatoes, then," she said, slipping into his casual tone.

"Exactly."

Brian laughed. "You see? He's humble, too. He's not even mentioning his novel."

Annie thought she might have caught Flynn glaring at his friend.

"The one that earned me nearly enough for a sack of groceries?" he asked. "Why mention it at all?"

"See, there's no living with him," Brian said to Annie.

A server waiting in line at the service bar turned and joined the conversation. "You're the infamous Daniel Flynn, right?" she asked.

"I am."

"Why don't you let us hear if you're as awful at music as Brian has been saying."

Flynn smiled, but didn't budge. "Worse, I promise."

"One song," she wheedled.

"Go on," Annie said. "I'll talk business while you're gone."

"I'd rather you did it in front of me," he said, but allowed himself to be dragged off all the same.

"So you've not heard Daniel play?" Brian asked.

"No." Between the writing and the university education, Annie wasn't sure she was ready to, either. She'd had Flynn nicely pigeonholed, but he'd flown the coop.

"Come on," Brian said. "We'll find a spot toward the front." He signaled one of the staff over and asked him to bring some chairs. As Annie and Brian were cutting through the throng, he said over his shoulder, "Daniel told me that old Hal Donovan has decided to start a pub chain."

"That's the general plan."

"And here I am consorting with the enemy." Laughing, he shook his head. "Only for Daniel Flynn."

They had worked their way up to the musicians' area. The waiter arrived, carrying two low stools over his head. He set them just outside of the circle, next to a table that held a clutter of the musicians' drinks.

Brian nodded his thanks to his employee. They sat, Annie facing the circle, and Brian, more angled away. She did her best to keep her attention trained on Brian, but it was a losing battle. She watched as Flynn took an offered fiddle, gave his thanks to the owner, then turned away from the circle of musicians and well, fiddled, she guessed, until satisfied that he knew the instrument.

"'Miss Monaghan's Reel'," he said to the others in the circle.

Everybody readied. Daniel began to tap out a rhythm, then started to play. After a few moments, the other musicians joined in. Annie, who had quit piano lessons after three miserable years, was floored. Flynn wasn't one of those cheesy fake-a-few-songs-to-get-the-girls-hot dabblers that she recalled from college. He could *really* play.

Other than a short-lived phase at age fifteen, she had never considered "groupie" as a career path. As she watched Flynn—and watched the other women in the area watch Flynn...*bitches*—Annie did some serious re-thinking. The pay wouldn't be all that great, but she had a feeling that the fringe benefits would sweeten the deal. Considerably.

"Annie?"

She dragged her focus from just over Brian's shoulder to his face. "Yes?"

"I was asking how quickly you turn tables in one of Donovan's restaurants."

"Oh...fifteen minutes, I think."

"*Fifteen?*"

Annie winced when she realized what she'd said. She'd never acted this unprofessionally, not even during endless management meetings when she fantasized about using fat black binder clips to clamp shut Hal's sons' mouths.

"Sorry, I misspoke. I meant fifty. And I should warn you, pubs and food service in general aren't exactly my areas of expertise. I'm more about analyzing industry numbers and trends. I've kind of been drafted into this particular project."

"Ah, I see. Well, we're a bit slower turning tables

here, but with our drink revenues, we're glad to let them sit and listen to the entertainment. Have you thought about bringing in some J1s?"

She was pretty sure she'd read about that on another restaurant's Web site while cyber-pub-surfing over the weekend. "Students on visas, right?"

He nodded. "Exactly. Come summer, you can have half your staff Irish. There's nothing like a bit of added color."

Annie's gaze wandered back to Flynn. He'd segued from one song to the next. This one followed the same beat, yet was a little sharper, a little more wry. He glanced her way and their gazes locked.

Yes, added color was a fine, fine thing.

When she looked back to Brian, another pub employee was there, saying something to him in low tones. Brian stood.

"Sorry, but I've got a bit of a situation to tend to," he said to Annie. "Why don't you and Daniel come by tomorrow around two? I'll take you through the kitchen, and we can talk some more about what it is you're wanting to do."

"That would be great," Annie said. And hopefully by tomorrow she would have gotten hold of herself, since what she was "wanting to do" right now involved Flynn exclusively and would definitely fall under the category of "too much information" if she shared the news with Brian Naughton.

The song ended. Flynn called out, "And that was 'Ms. Annie's Reel'."

The smile he then gave her was intimate, knowing, and scared the hell out of her. The truth was inescapable—when it came to Daniel Flynn, Annie was growing weak-kneed, up-against-the-wall easy.

8

If it was Thursday—and Annie wouldn't bet the farm on it—this must be Seattle.

Wednesday had been endless. Daniel had given her an o'dark in the morning wake-up call, then kept her running—and continually clueless about their plans—until three in the morning. He'd brought her to a rough south-side social club where beer, neighborhood gossip and city politics were the specials of the day. They had returned to Mulvaney's, where she'd conducted a what-would-you-do-differently-if-you-had-designed-this-pub? interview with Brian Naughton, while Daniel had chatted up the bar customers.

She'd visited an Irish dance school with harried moms waiting in one room and kids hammering away on hard shoes in the next. That night had been spent at two restaurants and three different bars, one of which was Korean, forcing Annie to accept that she would never find the common link in Flynn's secret itinerary.

In the course of their travels, she'd met a judge, sanitation workers, the manager of a five-star hotel, a woman Annie remained convinced was a high-priced call girl and a group of musicians just over from Ireland.

When she'd returned to her hotel room for what rest their next day's flight schedule would permit, she'd been relieved to see her missing suitcase, but too tired for real rejoicing. As she'd tossed around in bed waiting for sleep to come, two things had ground at her.

Tops on the list was the way it seemed that Flynn had done everything short of duct-taping someone to his side to avoid being alone with her. Granted, she might simply be wallowing in a little stress-induced paranoia. It wasn't often she felt like a stranger in her own damn country.

And that was gripe number two. Daniel knew more people in a city thousands of miles from his home than she knew back in Ann Arbor. Her last waking thought had been that she really needed to get out of the office more.

After a miserable night's rest, she'd been semilucid on the trip to the airport and dead out—not to mention probably drooling in her sleep—on the plane. Now, as she and Daniel rode in the back of a cab to their downtown Seattle bed-and-breakfast, she thumbed through pages of a travel guide in hopes of creating the illusion of security in her surroundings.

Really, though, she felt like a refugee—tired, poor and yearning to huddle somewhere. She half wondered whether he'd run her into the ground just so she couldn't obsess over the flight. If so, she owed him major thanks. And he owed her about twelve hours of downtime.

The cab slowed, then pulled to the curb. Annie looked out at a row of fairly worn-out looking retail spaces, dotted with the occasional gentrified gallery or shop.

"Is this the right place?" she asked Daniel, since he'd told her earlier that he'd asked Mrs. D. to book them here.

He checked a slip of paper. "It is. There's the door," he added, pointing to one inset between two shops. "The bed-and-breakfast is above the book store."

"*Adult* book store," she clarified.

Flynn was nearly whistling a happy tune. "Have faith, Annie."

It must be painful, being that optimistic all the time.

Once the cabbie had been paid, Flynn hefted their suitcases from the trunk. With her new clothing purchases added to the packing scheme, she'd had to sit on both her carry-on and her regular bag to close them. She knew that she should probably have thrown out some of her old stuff, but she just couldn't bring herself to do it. She grabbed the carry-on. In the spirit of letting Flynn feel macho—not that there seemed to be much evidence of risk to the contrary—she let him haul the bigger bags.

The dimly lit and ancient elevator groaned under their collective weight, but survived the trip to the second floor. Once there, Annie saw the light—literally.

Leaving her luggage just outside the elevator, she walked to a bank of windows that gave an incredible view over the rooftops and to Elliott Bay, just a few blocks west. To her left was the classic red Public Market sign for Pike Place Market, perched on the building's roof. She smiled at the sight, remembering how she'd sighed over *Sleepless in Seattle* as a dateless, movie-addicted college freshman.

"How'd you hear about this place?" she asked as she walked back toward Flynn, who she had to admit was looking a little worse for the wear, himself. His smile was marginally less cocky and his normally vivid blue eyes seemed somehow subdued.

"A friend of a friend," he said with a shrug.

Annie sensed a sort of "Six Degrees of Kevin Bacon" game in the offing, but her brain was too mushy to get a handle on it.

While Flynn kicked back on a sofa in the sitting area, she registered. Since it was before official check-in time, she tried to muzzle her sniveling when the innkeeper told her that their rooms wouldn't be ready for another couple of hours.

Once their luggage was safely stowed in the B and B's little office, she wandered over to the blue corduroy sofa that Flynn had been occupying. He'd charmed the innkeeper into letting him check his e-mail on the office computer, which Annie figured would take hours, given the man's popularity. At least she'd gained some nap time.

She tested the sofa's cushions with both palms. Content with its possibilities, she settled in. She had just wriggled into optimum comfort position when Flynn seized her ankles and swung her feet back to the ground.

"No, you don't," he said, immediately sitting next to her and eliminating the possibility that she could stretch out again. "I let you sleep on the plane, and that was bad enough."

"Come on, Flynn. Give me a break." She was whining, and she never whined. Bitched, maybe.

"You need to get your body clock straightened round. If you don't, you'll be up till dawn."

"I don't suppose it would help to point out that you're probably going to have me up until dawn anyway?"

"Not a bit." He stood, grabbed both her hands and hauled her up. "Till tonight, we're going to treat you as a concussion victim and keep you moving."

It seemed cheesy to ply her limited—and currently pretty ripe—physical charms on this guy, but she was desperate. And just maybe he was tired enough to get sucked in. Annie ran a hand up Flynn's chest. He felt so damn strong and good beneath her palm that she almost forgot she was in wheedle mode.

"Not even a little nap?"

He settled his hand over hers and drew it toward his mouth. "Not so much the closing of one eye."

No problem, since Annie's susceptible heart had started to race. His mouth was hot against her palm, and his kiss was slow enough that while reaction zinged from skin to nerve to brain, the rest of her bland dating life passed in front of her eyes. At least she'd have one decent memory to take with her. And when he released her hand, Annie knew there was an excellent chance she'd never sleep again.

IT WAS A PERILOUS and slippery slope from kissing Annie's hand to kissing the countless other places Daniel had taken to speculating about. And he'd been fool enough to begin the slide.

Luck and schedule had been his allies yesterday. He'd had little time alone with Annie and thus little time to cave to temptation. But just now he'd love to throw the back cushions off that sofa and curl up with her in his arms, not really caring a dog's arse about the B and B's other customers. Because that would be wrong for Annie—and for him—it was time to move.

"Hungry?" he asked.

She nodded. "A little."

"Let's visit the market, then."

"Don't you ever get tired?"

She didn't know the half of it. Fighting the urge to have her was one bloody exhausting battle.

They left the B and B, then cut through Post Alley to

the market itself. It was nearly eleven, and the place teemed with even more people than products.

"Let's take a look, then try a restaurant," he said to Annie.

She agreed, so on they walked.

Daniel was blissfully distracted by the color, scents and variety. Row after row of silvery-scaled fish bordering produce and then into candles, honey, flowers, touristy odds and ends and—*hello, what have we here?*—an entire store devoted to condoms. To be sure, they sold them in Ireland, but not with quite the same happy abandon.

"Can we please move along?" Annie said as he lingered at the display.

He glanced over at her. "So who do you think buys the striped ones?"

"Clowns."

"And the glow-in-the-dark?"

"The visually impaired."

"And the giant one, any thoughts there?"

An unwilling smile tugged at the corners of her mouth. "Do you want to go inside and check out the stock? Think you could make me blush more that way?"

He brushed the hair away from her perfect shell of an ear. "That couple in the room next to yours at the Almont, Annie, what kind would they be buying?"

"Spiked," she replied, then strolled away.

Daniel stood there, only the fact that the air had left his lungs stopping him from laughing. He'd been accused of many things in his day, but he'd never been mistaken for a buyer of spiked condoms. Life around Annie Rutherford was a brilliant thing. He'd truly miss her when the time came to leave.

When he'd checked his e-mail earlier, amid all the spam regarding miracle growth to parts he was already reasonably content with, there had waited some real news. The most alarming was a quick message from his friend Aislinn, telling him that James and Da had gotten in an argument, and James had stormed off and taken a job at a hotel in Salthill, leaving the family short-handed at the pub.

Daniel knew he couldn't move on just yet. Since he'd arrived, his talks with Hal had taken an odd turn. It seemed that for all the older man said, more was going unspoken. Perhaps in a few weeks, Daniel could unravel the question of truly why he'd been brought to Ann Arbor. It damn well wasn't all about pubs. Once he understood and had done what he could to help Hal, he'd be free to go home.

But then there'd also been a tempting note. One of his New York friends had had enough of city life. He was giving notice at work and planned to start an eco-touring company with his girlfriend in Belize. Paul and Meri wondered whether Daniel would be willing to pitch in, and he could nearly see himself doing it.

Steps ahead, Annie was picking her way through a table filled with souvenirs, including, God help her kitchen, a selection of Space Needle salt-and-pepper shakers. He wasn't sure what purpose the bizarre structure continued to serve in Seattle, let alone in Annie's kitchen. For the sake of diplomacy, he took his time catching up to her.

As he did, Daniel tried to ignore the market's press of tourists that grew stronger as lunchtime approached. To him, this was nearly intolerable, and life in New York unthinkable. He could understand why, after five years,

Paul and Meri would now want to move to a slower pace. In their shoes, he'd be asylum bound.

"Flynn," Annie called. "What do you think of these?" She held aloft a pair of the shakers.

"Grand," he said, managing not to grimace too horribly.

His effort was worth the smile he received in return. Even tired, grumpy and frayed around the edges, Annie Rutherford was the prettiest woman he'd seen in some time. And since kissing her would be a fool's act, he bought those howlingly ugly salt-and-pepper shakers instead. A fool's act, too, but safer by miles than another kiss.

THIS MORNING, DANIEL FLYNN had bought her a gift. Okay, so it wasn't expensive or sentimental, but even hours after sunset, Annie couldn't lose the involuntary smile that had settled on her face. She knew she was no better—and probably even worse—than the other women who were total tongue-draggers in his presence. But, hey, she had the Space Needle set and they didn't.

Before heading out for the evening, she'd also been given the luxury of a little time to fuss over her appearance, even if it had been in one of the B and B's shared baths. Flynn, it turned out, had been unknowingly upgraded to a suite on the third floor. He'd offered his facilities, but the implied intimacy had been more than Annie could handle.

Tonight, she wore an amber-and-ivory flirty little dress that she'd picked up in Chicago. It was short enough that her legs didn't look stumpy, yet just long enough that her every thought wasn't consumed by just how high it might ride.

Good thing, too, since Flynn had made her get behind the bar and learn to draw pints at their first stop, a small bar just off Pioneer Square, which of course had been owned by one of Flynn's countless "friends of a friend." She'd bowed out of the stout business when the dinner rush had started. Strappy, high-heeled sandals and the round drainage holes in bar mats didn't coexist well.

Dinner had been more like a party, with fourteen people at a long table swapping jokes and stories. Daniel had been wonderful and funny and so clearly interested in everyone. Annie had tried to keep up, but she had a soft voice that refused to carry in a crowd. Besides, she was so punchy with lack of sleep that she really didn't trust herself not to say something totally off-the-wall.

Now, she and Flynn sat at the bar of another pub, this one nearly beneath their bed-and-breakfast, looking out onto the row of shops and restaurants lining Post Alley.

Annie looked around. "Why do you think Hal wants this so much?"

Daniel glanced her way. He seemed to have been checking out his neighbor's cigarette. As casual as ever, he gave a shrug that was no more than a brief raise of his left shoulder. "To grow his business, I suppose."

"You can cross that one off the list. As far as business decisions go, this is about as bad as one can get." She sipped at her stout, wrinkling her nose at the taste. It was like drinking a loaf of dark, lead-based bread. "I think maybe he's delayed his midlife crisis until now. Back when he would have been scheduled to have it, one of his sons went off the deep end."

"Ah, Rob," Flynn said.

"He told you about him?"

Daniel nodded.

Annie stared into her pint, not sure what to make of this. Hal never spoke of Rob, his eldest son. Annie only knew because Sasha had told her the tale of her wild uncle Rob, who'd cashed out of the family business back when she'd been a kid.

He'd taken the money his dad had given him, moved to Florida, partied hard, then left the planet in a *Miami Vice* blaze of glory, totaling a cigarette racer into about a billion tiny pieces. According to Sasha, family lore had it that her grandfather had turned into a total hard-ass after that.

Annie frowned, thinking of the two unanswered messages she'd left for Sasha today. Thirteen years of friendship couldn't possibly fizzle in a week. At least, she was pretty sure of that.

"You're not liking your pint?" Daniel asked, pulling her back from an incipient case of the blues.

Annie looked at him. Up close, it was hard to miss his thick lashes. They weren't curly, but so lush that it was a crime for a guy to have them.

"I'm more of a fluffy-drink girl," she replied.

"I think we need to be broadening your horizons."

"They're plenty broad already, thanks."

"Then you can tell me the difference between Irish whiskey and Scotch?"

"Their island of origin?" She figured it was a smart-assed answer, but one hard to refute.

"True, but sadly vague."

"It's as good as you're getting."

"And you expect me to bring you back to Hal with your Irish education lacking?"

"It works for me. I never drink hard liquor. I hate the taste of it."

"How would you know if you've never drunk it?

Rory," Flynn said to the bartender, "let's have a top-shelf tasting—Irish, Scotch and single malt."

The bartender nodded and began setting up small shots of liquor in glasses. Beneath each glass he placed a cocktail napkin on which he'd written the brand name. And the row of those names was beginning to stretch out too long for Annie's comfort.

"Flynn…"

"Trust me," he said.

The scary thing was, she *had* begun to sort of trust him. Of course, that was news she didn't need to share. "Right. You're not the one who's facing a night before the white porcelain god."

He leaned forward and grabbed an empty pint glass from beneath the counter. "Sip, then spit."

As if she really wanted Daniel Flynn watching her spit.

"Now, here we go. There are three differences between Scotch and Irish whiskey. First, Irish is triple-distilled, which makes it smoother. Second, we don't go roasting our barley over a peat fire, so you won't taste smoke in Irish whiskey. Third—and this is the important one—no matter what those wee Scot bastards say, the Irish invented whiskey."

"Along with arrogance, huh?"

Daniel laughed. "Start with this one," he said, handing her a glass. "Smell it, as if it were a fine wine."

She did her best not to roll her eyes. The whiskey was a pretty color, almost matching one of the shades of deep amber in her new dress, but she'd never been the sort of fool to buy her drinks to match her dress. At least, not in a long, long time.

Annie sniffed at the glass's contents. "It's actually kind of nice," she said to Flynn. "Nearly sweet."

She sipped, then clutched the bar's edge. *Gasoline.* She'd just swallowed stinkin' gasoline. She squeezed her eyes shut as her brain seized up, barraged with competing mental commands of *"swallow!" "gag!"* and *"spit!"*

"Annie?" She could feel Daniel's hand close over hers. "Try a drink of water, love."

Love.

Shock at his word choice got the whiskey down, but it was a damn close call. After chugging the water, she looked at him through teary eyes, and got one of his smiles.

"It's an acquired taste, but once it's yours, there's nothing better," he said.

She knew that he was referring to the whiskey, but a foolish, greedy voice inside Annie whispered, *"He could be talking about you."*

Totally panicked, Annie lifted the next glass in the tasting row. That foolish, greedy voice was about to go brain-deep in Irish gasoline.

DANIEL WAS HAVING a hard time grasping the particulars of the event, but it appeared that Annie had just invited herself into his room. After switching on the lights, Daniel checked his watch—past two in the morning. Perhaps he'd done too fine a job in keeping Annie moving. She seemed to have danced straight on into the next day.

Already, she prowled his suite. "My room's nice, but besides the nonexistent bathroom, I also don't have a kitchen, or a huge living room…" She pulled back the drapes. "Or a balcony!"

She slipped outside before he could catch up to her. Daniel counted to ten, hoping she'd have the sense to come inside on her own. When she didn't, he uttered a string of his finest Irish obscenities and joined Ms. Annie outside.

She was leaning over the railing at what he considered a life-endangering angle. If he weren't so damn worried for her, he might have better enjoyed the ripe curve of her bottom.

"It's starting to rain. You might be wanting to come inside," he suggested.

She looked back over her shoulder, but didn't budge. "Hey, there. Great view you've got, but it's really a long way down."

He edged a step closer, thinking he stood no risk of dying a brave man.

Annie slipped one foot between the balcony's bars. Daniel forced himself not to show his panic. After all, it was *his* bloody phobia and he didn't need to go sharing it.

"Do you ever have daydreams about what you'd do in an emergency situation?" she asked, one hand swinging casually into that long drop to a hard landing. "I mean, suppose there was a fire. Would you have the guts to jump?"

Not likely. He did manage to will himself one more step forward.

"You might want to try the fire ladder," he said, looping an arm around her waist and drawing her back from the wrought-iron rail.

"Good point," she said ever so cheerfully. "I must be slipping. I always check each new place I'm in for the emergency exits." She walked to the side of the balcony where the ladder was bolted on, then patted it. "Good thing to have, you know?"

Annie clearly had no fear of heights to go with her fear of flying. He, on the other hand, imagined paradise as a very flat place, one with no balconies or views from skyscraper windows.

"Wow, it's raining," she said, finally noticing. She held out one hand to catch some drops. "Let's go inside."

Which, just now, was close enough to paradise for Daniel. Especially with Annie in it.

"I'm still not sure about that whiskey thing," she said. "I'll agree that the Irish stuff was better than the Scotch, though."

"Diplomatic of you," he replied, trailing after her as she stepped into the kitchen area and began opening the cupboard doors.

"I think I probably should have eaten some more tonight. If I add up my meals since Tuesday, it's looking kind of like a twisted spa regime." She moved to the fridge and rattled about. "Empty, dammit."

Annie gave up on her kitchen hunt and walked a circle around him, instead. "If I weren't starved and tired and probably a little too buzzed, I'd be smart enough to shut up now, but I'm not. So...name your price, Daniel Flynn. What would it take to have you teach me to be like you?"

9

DANIEL FLYNN NEVER stammered, stumbled or tripped on his tongue. Except now.

"Like—like me?"

"Yes, like you," Annie repeated, as if it were the most patently obvious concept on earth.

"Annie, you *don't* want to be like me."

"Come on, everybody loves you. People hardly notice me."

"*I* notice you."

She laughed. "That's because I've been in your face eighty percent of every day."

"But you've been in my mind one hundred percent," he said.

She blinked, swaying slightly. "Impossible."

Daniel shook his head. Now wasn't the time to be having this conversation. He wanted her with not even the almost shot of whiskey she'd managed to gag down during their tasting. But they were here, now, and he could take no more of her diminished ego. Whoever had parted Annie from her confidence deserved to turn on a slow spit in hell.

He took her by the hand and led her to the raised area of the suite that held the bedroom. Daniel didn't switch on the lamp that would have lit the space, leaving it only in a soft wash of light from the kitchen and living room lights. He drew Annie next to him, by the full-length oval mirror in its footed frame.

"Stand in front of me."

She did as he asked, but he noted the way her gaze skittered away from the mirror, locking instead on the bed nearby.

"I want you to look in the mirror with me."

She took a step to her right. "I think I've changed my mind. How about if we just skip the whole be-like-you idea and hop on over to the bed? Are those down pillows? They definitely look like it."

Daniel wrapped his arms around her waist, drawing her back. He leaned down and spoke softly in her ear. "You started this. The mirror, Annie."

She shivered.

"You want to know how to be more like me?"

"Yes." Her expression was so serious that his heart ached just a bit for her.

"Then I suppose the first thing you need to do is build one bastard of an ego."

She laughed.

"I'm not joking, Annie me girl." He smiled. "Well, at least not much. Once you stop worrying about yourself, the rest will come easier."

"Right. Like you've ever worried about yourself. You've probably been a god among men forever."

"A god?" It was definitely his turn to laugh. "It's a grand compliment, but you've yet to see me before my morning coffee, or when someone is fool enough to interrupt me while I'm writing."

"Spare me the humility, okay?"

He smiled, sifting the silk of her brown hair between

his fingertips. "I reached this height at fourteen and nearly lacked the skin to cover my bones. By the time my mam had fattened me enough that she didn't have to worry about the neighbors whispering that I was being starved, I'd turned into a nasty git." He paused and laughed. "I suppose most boys that age do. Anyway, I was none too happy with myself, but now I am…and I'm going to let you in on my secret. Would you look in the mirror, *please?*"

She frowned, but at least she was looking. "This had better be good."

"I want you to repeat after me, 'I, Annie Rutherford, am witty, wise and beautiful.'"

"Good one, Flynn. Sorry, but no can do."

He shook his head. "Positive thinking. You're not seeing yourself right. Try it for me…'I, Annie Rutherford—'"

She turned in his embrace, twined her arms around his neck and kissed him. Daniel had to admit to an instantaneous and nearly staggering surge of lust when her tongue flicked against his lower lip, but damned if he'd let her dance around this moment with kisses.

No, he'd take this one on account and demand more later. Once she was seeing herself as he saw her.

"A fine try," he said after he'd found the strength to move his mouth from hers. "Brilliant, almost."

He gently turned her back toward the mirror. "Do you know how incredible you looked when you told Hal Donovan just where you were drawing the line? You took my breath away, Annie Rutherford. And when you were pulling those pints at the pub tonight, as though the world depended on your being perfect? It made me want you more."

Her gray eyes were wide now, nearly with shock, he'd say.

"But do you know when I find you most beautiful? It's when you think no one's watching and you're looking about, watching everything. Nothing much gets by you, Annie, and that makes me hungry for you in ways you wouldn't believe."

"Flynn…"

He heard the uncertainty in her voice.

"I'd never lie to you. Now, will you say it for me?"

"I, Annie Rutherford, am witty—" She shook her head. "This is so lame. How can you ever expect me to believe this?"

He gave her the simplest truth of all. "Because I do."

"Bull."

He knew the softness beneath the tough-girl talk. Reaching in front of her, he untied the thin bit of ribbon that held the fabric gathered at her dress's low neckline. "Something about you has me curious, though." He slipped just one fingertip beneath the cloth and touched her skin. "Will I find more freckles here?" He ventured in a bit, tracing the lacy edge of her bra. "Or under this?"

She leaned back against him, and he wondered whether she could feel the pounding of his heart. It nearly matched the beat of hers beneath his fingers.

"You're beautiful, Annie, inside and out."

"Why are you doing this?"

Unable to fight temptation any longer, he slipped his hand fully beneath her scrap of a bra. Her nipple rose against his palm.

"I'm doing this for selfish reasons," he said, amazed that his voice didn't break like a spotty adolescent's. "Because I want you happy."

Her eyes closed, and she traced her fingers over the back of his hand.

"Say it, Annie. Please."

He watched as her lips began to shape the first word. "I… Annie Rutherford, am witty, wise and beautiful."

"Yes," he said, unable to fight back a smile. "That, you are."

He withdrew his hand just enough to rub his fingertips over that hard little nipple. Her eyes came open, and their gazes met in the mirror.

"It's not fair, pressuring me like this."

He'd have taken her words for a complaint, except her mouth had a definite upward curve.

One brush of his fingertips, then another. Her breath was coming faster, and he was harder than he'd been since age thirteen when, on holiday in Spain with his family, he'd spied on a group of college girls sunbathing topless.

"This is pressure?" he managed to say.

"Um…duress, maybe?"

Parts of Daniel were under undeniable duress. He slid his free hand down to her tummy and drew her fully into contact with him.

"What you're feeling isn't even close," he said.

Her smile grew with her awareness of his state. "Want to count my freckles?"

Though it was the last thing he'd expected to hear tonight, it was also the very best. They could have their bit of fun—not carry it so far that his conscience objected, yet still maybe ease the hunger that had been riding him.

Being a big man was something he took for granted, except at moments like this. The ability to easily scoop Annie into his arms, and to turn and carry her to the bed, wiped the slate clean of every childhood taunt he'd taken.

She lay against the lime-and-yellow-striped bed-spread. With her dress nearly matching the golds and browns in her hair, she looked like one of his favorite caramel sweets.

"Take off your shirt," she commanded.

Fine, then, a caramel with a bit of a bite.

Daniel began to work the shirt's buttons and was ready to shrug out of it when she said, "Hang on."

She rolled onto her side and, elbow bent, propped her head on her hand. "Move over in front of the mirror, and turn to face it."

An equitable demand, he supposed. He walked the few steps until he was directly between Annie and the mirror. She resettled a bit, then said, "Now I get you coming and going."

She might, indeed.

Daniel made short work of the shirt, watching her watch him in the mirror.

"Time to start counting," she said.

In the instant it had taken him to turn back, she'd begun to try to pull down the bedspread and lose her sandals at the same time. Daniel reached out and rid her of the footwear. They landed bedside with a soft thud. He discarded his shoes, as well, then joined her.

"Where to begin?" he mused.

She raised one leg and waggled her foot in the air. "Here?"

"As good a place as any," he said, sliding downward to grasp her ankle.

And so he began to count, using kisses as markers on each freckle he found. Perhaps there'd been none behind her knee, but he'd been pleased to find that with just a wee nip, he could work both laughter and a gasp from her.

A few kisses more brought him to the ivory-white of her inner thigh. A glimpse above that, to damp, silky bronze-colored panties. The sight was a reeling blow to his self-control. Daniel moved upward, settling his mouth over hers and letting his tongue, at least, have a shadow of the full pleasure that he'd not be allowing himself tonight.

Damn, but she kissed as though she'd take the whole of him inside her, if she could. He settled between her legs and pressed his erection against her, because if he didn't, he'd go mad. Even with the layers of clothes still keeping him from her, the pleasure was enough to make him groan.

Annie wove her fingers into his hair and rocked hard against him, once, twice, then once more.

"I want to be on top."

Of course she did. He rolled to the other side of the bed, and she knelt above him, straddling him.

She smiled. "Better." She shimmied her way out of her dress and sent it sailing to the floor, which Daniel found a surprise, and a ball-tightening one at that.

He ran one hand over the lush curve of her hips. She was no skin-and-bones Annie, which was a grand thing, since he'd never been so damn starved for a woman. He moved back on the bed enough that he could lean on the headboard. Once he'd resettled, she came forward and kissed him.

The kiss grew until his heart pounded like a madman's, and the need for full body-to-body contact was nearly too much to fight. Daniel eased her back until she was riding him.

"Let me look at you," he said.

He thought she might protest, but again she shocked

him, for she levered up, unhooked her bra and sent it to the carpet, too. He was a man, and fully possessed of the male guidance system that led his hands immediately to her breasts.

Annie looked down. "Not much to write home about, are they?"

"They're perfect, though not the sort of thing I'd be sharing with my brothers anyway." *Or anyone else on the planet*, he thought with a surge of utterly unaccustomed possessiveness.

And her breasts were perfect, too. Not large, to be sure, but they fit the rest of her so ideally. And the fit to his hands wasn't bad, either.

Daniel had to taste her. Sliding his hands round to her back and drawing her toward him, he brought one nipple to his mouth.

God, yes. Warm and faintly perfumed…an early summer Saturday afternoon…

Annie gasped, but since she'd bracketed his head between her hands and held him to her, he was guessing that her pleasure was as intense as his.

"We look amazing," she whispered.

Daniel let go of perfection just long enough to turn his head. She was watching the two of them in the mirror. Hard became infinitely harder as he looked, too.

"We do."

She took his hand and settled it low on her belly. "Touch me here."

He did, and had to set his jaw against the need that slammed through him. He slid two fingers beneath the damp panel of silk between her legs, through the wet curls that guarded her, and into sleek heat.

She gasped a *yes!*

Daniel started a rhythm that he knew would please her, even if it made him forever crippled by lack of release. Before he would have thought it possible, and damn well before he was through watching her, she gasped and cried out his name. He knew a deep satisfaction that it was his first name, too.

"Go with it, love," he murmured, easing her through the moment.

Soon she lay limp, nearly boneless, against him. Daniel settled into the pillows, his heart still slamming and the fit of his denims nearly agony. On an intellectual level, he wasn't a believer in easy sex and fast and inevitable goodbyes. But it wasn't his intellect paining him just now, was it?

Daniel closed his eyes and thought of Annie, of how she already seemed to be dealing with enough in her life, and how she might not know what she truly wanted.

Noble, yes.

Helpful, no.

"Wow," she said as her breathing slowed.

He smiled despite his discomfort. "That would be a word for it."

"Sorry I was so…um…fast. It's not usually like that for me."

He settled a hand on the round curve of her bum. "That's as mad as apologizing for your breasts."

"Ha!"

Daniel waited for the argument to follow the scoff, but just maybe he'd loved the fight out of her. For now, at least. Still holding her close, he tried to concentrate on something other than his raging arousal. Say, perhaps, the number of stripes on the clown condoms back in the market, or…

She settled her hand at the top of his jeans, her fingers winnowing beneath the waistband. Daniel sucked in a breath, willing those smart fingers lower.

"I want to come again," she said, "but this time I want you inside me."

His eyes opened with a jolt. Forget the woman not knowing what she wanted. He'd be a fool to argue against her command, except there were still twenty-first century matters to be considered. First, he kissed her hard, his tongue tangling with hers. Then he addressed the essentials.

"Before this goes another step, I'll tell you I'm clean, Annie. And you, have you been tested?"

"Passed all my tests two months ago," she said, running her fingertip down the fly of his jeans. "It's the only A-plus I ever consistently get, but it's a biggie."

"Right, then. I'll be right back, love," he said, then moved from the bed while he still had the willpower to do so.

She stretched and sighed. "Hurry."

In the bathroom, Daniel fumbled his way through his travel kit until he found the small box of condoms at the bottom. He didn't look in the mirror, didn't pause long enough to ask himself what the hell he was doing, letting matters with Annie run this wild. He simply grabbed the box and left his conscience behind.

He switched off the few lights that were on in the suite, then partially closed the curtains over the balcony door, allowing just enough of the city's glow inside to find his way back to Annie. Once bedside, he dropped the condom box on the nightstand and shucked his socks and jeans.

Daniel moved next to her on the mattress, drifting a

line of kisses up one arm and then to her lips. Annie, however, was lacking in enthusiasm. Or any response at all, actually.

He pulled away a bit. "Annie?"

She sighed and snuggled deeper into the pillows. It appeared that after incinerating his good intentions, she had fizzled out. Torn between laughter and pounding his head against the floor, Daniel settled for pulling the sheet and blanket to gently snoring Ms. Annie's chin, then sleeping himself.

ANNIE SLOWLY WOKE. Even before opening her eyes, a few disturbing matters became apparent. First, she wasn't alone, and second, she was feeling far too much sheet against her skin to have slept in her favorite boxers and T-shirt.

Last night hovered in the outer reaches of her memory, accessible only after major caffeine ingestion. Even without details, she knew that the happy whistling she was hearing came from Flynn. She also knew it wasn't reasonable to be annoyed with a guy for being cheerful, but that didn't make her feel any less cranky.

What reason could he have to be so damn glad?

Then the nearly naked motivation hit her.

She cleared her throat the best she could and croaked, "Flynn?"

Pans rattled and the whistling continued.

She peeled open one eye. Yes, this definitely was Daniel's suite and not her tiny room. Clad in jeans and a black shirt, he was down in the kitchen area. His back was to her as he reached into the refrigerator.

"Flynn?"

He turned, smiling. "Last night, you were calling me Daniel. Would you like some coffee? I've been to the market and have all we need for breakfast. Unless you'd like to join the other guests in the dining room, that is." He checked his watch. "There still might be time."

"I don't want to talk about food."

"Good enough."

Annie sat up, clutching the sheet to her chest. A grinding ache made itself known in her head. "How much did I drink last night?"

"Nearly a full shot of whiskey, I'm guessing."

Which pretty much left her in the featherweight division of whiskey-drinkers. "Did we...uh—"

"Oversleep? Yes. You did, at least. I've been up a while. It's nearly ten now."

"No, I was more wondering if—"

"I've a hair of the dog to put in your coffee?"

He was enjoying this. "No. I was wondering if we had sex, and you damn well know that's what I wanted to ask."

"True," he said. "But why should I rush the pleasure of hearing you ask?"

"So?"

His smile stretched wider. "So?"

"Did we?"

"At the risk of sounding arrogant, if we had, that's not a question you'd need to be asking. Though we did come close." He reached down and pulled a skillet from a lower cupboard. "If you look on the bench at the foot of the bed, you'll find your bags. I was thinking you wouldn't mind if I borrowed your room key."

Giving dignity up for lost, she scooted to the end of the bed. Kneeling, she dug through her suitcase, all the while trying to pin the sheet over assets she knew he'd already seen.

And touched.

And tasted.

Right after she'd confessed that she wanted to be just like him. Yes, it was all coming back in too-vivid detail.

Were her hands shaking? No more whiskey, ever again.

"Why don't you have a shower and get yourself ready for the day?" Flynn called from the kitchen. "By the time you're out, I'll have food for you."

She already felt as though she'd swallowed a big, fat case of the guilts, and she wasn't exactly sure why she felt that way. "I'll skip the food thing if you don't mind."

"I'm cooking all the same."

Annie worked up a borderline-adolescent *whatever*, gave up on the sheet as camouflage, grabbed her stuff and staggered to the bathroom.

While she waited for the shower water to come to temperature, she dug through her toiletry bag for her lavender shampoo and some aspirin. Flynn's belongings were scattered across the counter, random but with definite style, like the man himself.

Annie located the aspirin, popped them into her mouth and bent to sip water from the cold tap. She stood and swallowed. While wiping the back of her hand across her mouth, she was captured by her reflection in the mirror.

God, she barely looked like herself! She wasn't sure if this was a good or a bad thing, but it sure as hell wasn't comfortable.

Her face was pinker than usual and her lips fuller. Her hair wasn't terminally straight, either. She supposed she could fob off the hair change on the Seattle humidity, but she knew it was from her everything-but-the-deed-itself night with Daniel Flynn.

He was, as she'd told Sasha, a walking invitation to go off task. And she'd already veered so far off her career path that having a global positioning system strapped to her ass wouldn't help her find the way back.

"Don't panic," she whispered to that wild reflection. "No panic."

But it was already too damn late for that. Panic was off and to the races.

10

IF DANIEL HAD slapped together a guy's sort of breakfast with fried eggs and bacon swimming in grease, Annie would have found it a lot easier to say what she had to. But no, he had gone the fresh-and-sugary route, which meant that on top of her panic, she had to battle the urge to scarf down everything he'd set out.

Still fussing with her wet hair, which she'd twisted and clipped at the back of her head, she lingered between the kitchen area and the table. Flynn stood in front of the oven. Unless her nose was as off as the rest of her, he was pulling out blueberry muffins.

"Did you make those?" she asked.

"Sorry, but I'm a reheat-only kind of chef."

Somehow, that didn't make her feel better. Taking a moment to get her brain back in the game, Annie walked to the small dining table. On it waited a few croissants, a bowl of raspberries and a plate with fresh melon slices in hues of pale green and sherbet-orange.

Annie's stomach grumbled. She had to get this over with. "About last night…" She trailed off, watching him juggle muffins from a misshapen tin that he must have found in the cupboard. His hand brushed against the metal's hot edge, and she heard him mutter a blunt phrase.

He was even a sexy klutz, and she was in deep trouble. She grabbed a croissant, tore off one pointy little end and popped it into her mouth. The rest she hoarded on her plate for future stress relief.

"You were saying?" Daniel prompted as he carried two fat muffins to the table.

Still chewing, she brushed past him and filled two slightly chipped green mugs with coffee, then returned. "Here's the thing. The way I acted last night was some sort of crazed reaction to travel. That wasn't me."

"You're sure about that?" he asked as he held out a chair for her.

She wanted to yank it from him and tell him to quit being so nice.

"Positive." The real Annie would never have flung herself at someone as together as Daniel Flynn. She always salvaged her guys from the scratch-and-dent bin.

She sat, and he soon settled opposite her. She let her brain switch off and her mouth go on autopilot. "We're going home today, and I'd appreciate it if we could leave behind everything that happened last night."

"Everything?"

"Yes. I don't think we should be so, um…personal with each other." She paused just long enough to nod her thanks as he placed a muffin on her plate. "I can't pinpoint why last night was wrong, but it was. I mean, it's not like I can say I shouldn't sleep with you because we're in the same office. You're a consultant and I'm pretty much a short-timer. But something just isn't working for me."

The smile he shot her way from over the rim of his mug carried a wealth of confidence and sensual awareness. Annie swallowed hard.

"I don't mean sexually," she said before he could point out the obvious. "I just mean that this is making me uncomfortable." She plucked some raspberries from the small bowl in the middle of the table and downed them, then broke her muffin in quarters. "So, no sex, okay?"

His utter calm made her palms grow a little clammy. Silence stretched out between them. The only noise in the suite came through the open balcony door. Somewhere below, a shopkeeper was sweeping the sidewalk. Without even looking, Annie knew that person was doing a better job at cleaning up a mess than she was. Still, she managed to keep her mouth shut and wait for Daniel to speak.

Finally, after a bite of croissant and some more coffee, he got back to her. "You're waiting for me to nod my head and give it a 'Yes, Annie,' aren't you?"

She picked the sugary top off a piece of muffin. "That would be the general idea."

"But I'm afraid the answer's no."

"No?"

"Unlike your other rules, this one's sadly lacking in detail."

"Come on, how much more specific can you get than 'no sex'?"

He laughed. "Love, you have a former president who wrapped himself all around that one."

"I'm not a politician, okay?" And she was pretty damn sure she wasn't his love, either.

"No, but let's be thinking about this executive order, just the same." He speared a narrow wedge of melon and set it on his plate. "See, it hits me even harder than your 'I'm the leader and you're the follower' speech. There, I might have been inclined to humor you, but this?" He shook his head. "How about we break down the 'no sex' bit?"

"Do what you have to, Flynn," she said, feigning a boredom that simply didn't exist.

He leaned back in his chair. "Let's say I kiss you—just a casual brush against the cheek—is that considered sex?"

"Of course not."

"And so you're saying that it's permitted?"

"I guess. But not in the office."

"Grand, then. Casual kisses are fair game. How about on the lips, Annie? No tongue, of course."

After last night's total abandon, his words shouldn't be making her blush, but they were. She picked up a cantaloupe slice and fit it to the curve of her croissant.

"No, that's not sex, either," she said without looking at him.

She heard the scrape of a chair.

"Be right back," he said. "I've a feeling I should be taking notes."

Annie watched as he dug though his bag and extracted a notebook and a fat black pen. He pulled the cap from it, and she saw it was a fountain pen, which struck her as romantic, somehow.

"Ready now," he said once he'd sat, pushed aside his plate and written *kiss—yes*. His script was a lefty's bold and angular scrawl, one more clue in the mystery-of-Flynn's-allure puzzle that she had no business solving.

"How about full-out snogging...you know, tongues and moans and what-have-you, like last night? If we had gone no further than that, would it have been sex?"

Before she could work up an answer, another bite of muffin had to die on the altar of Memories Best Forgotten.

"Technically, no, that's not sex, but it is a bad idea."

Pen scratched against paper. *Full snog—bad idea.*

"So now we've moved into a gray area," he said. "How about touching you? Will I be breaking your rules if I come round to your side of this table and put my hands under your top?"

Only an act of supreme will kept Annie from letting her eyes fall closed as she recalled the feel of his hands, hot and sure, against her skin. "Flynn, I— I don't know. All I know is that I can't sleep with you."

He capped his pen and set it on top of the notebook. "Would it shock you if I told you that until you persuaded me otherwise, I had no intention of letting it go beyond a bit of panting and groping last night?"

"Panting and *groping?*"

"To refresh your memory, you were panting, and I was taking care of the groping."

He'd given the best deadpan delivery she'd ever witnessed. "Are you trying to tick me off?"

"Why not? I'm bloody furious right now." He pushed away from the table and circled to her side. "I'm not some mindless bastard out for a rut, Annie."

He came down on his haunches and angled her chair so that she faced him. "I don't make love to a woman casually and I don't do it without thought. We haven't known each other long, but until this morning, I thought at least we knew each other well."

"I don't want to talk about this," she said, eyeing her waiting plate of food.

He laughed. "Of course you don't, *now*. You've given

your edict and what's left to be said?" He stood, then held out his hand to her.

Since she had no choice, Annie took it. He drew her to her feet. When she tried to reclaim her hand, he kept his fingers laced though hers.

"Be honest. Are you embarrassed?"

She wanted to tell him the truth—that she was scared out of her mind. That she'd never reacted to a guy the way she had last night. That even though it was a really bad idea, she was just easy enough to want to do it again this morning, and that's what had her stressed enough to visualize eating her way through Pike Place Market. But she'd already been too needy in front of him. She needed to regain her dignity.

"Embarrassed? Jeez, Flynn, I don't know. In fact, I don't know anything right now, and I figure that's as good a reason as any not to—to—"

"Make love?" he suggested.

"Okay. Make love."

"Then we won't."

She was definitely up for an award nomination in the category of Most Conflicted Chick, because once he'd agreed, Annie felt about two inches shorter from the emotional letdown.

"Until I'm sure you're a woman of your word," he added.

And Flynn was rising fast among the nominees for Most Able to Push Annie's Buttons.

"What's that supposed to mean?" she asked.

"Last night you told me just what you wanted…all the interesting details." He laughed, then gave her a lopsided smile. "Of course, you fell asleep right after. And this morning you've been everything in a woman that drives a man to murder, so I think I'm entitled to a bit of doubt. From here on, Annie, whatever happens between us is up to you."

Nice, but she'd been pretty sure that she had a vote already. She was about to remind him as much when he spoke again.

"Now, I'm an optimist," he said. "I figure that sooner or later, you'll decide to make love—sooner being the preferable timing. But just so I don't wake to another morning of Annie-remorse, I'll be wanting the words from you in writing."

She tugged her hand from his. "In writing? Like a contract?"

He winced as though she'd suggested something lethal. "*Contract?* No, too many endless obligations there. I'm thinking of it more as a moment to pause. If you can put it on paper, I'll know you mean it."

Annie mulled the concept. A written demand for sex… Weird, but the thought appealed to her. In fact, it was just kinky enough to make her toes curl, and in a good holding-all-power way, too.

"Any words in particular?" she asked, coloring her tone with some snarkiness, just so she was playing the game right.

Daniel laughed. "I'd be making it brief. No point in having me read too much when we could be getting on to better things."

"And if I don't feel like writing the words?"

He walked back to the table, paused and plucked a couple of raspberries from the bowl. "I begin to test those rules of yours. To see how well you bend."

"I don't." She lied, of course. When it came to guys, she'd made a career of contortionism—first a crisp conservative for her grad school money-hound boyfriends and then a green eco-warrior for Garth. Not this time, though. For matters of business and personal pride, she needed to keep on-task.

"Really?" he said, looking ripe for the challenge.

On the other hand, all work and no play made Annie a very cranky girl. She watched as Daniel popped one raspberry in his mouth and ate it. Then he strolled her way as though he had a leisurely day to arrive. Though he made for some fine viewing pleasure, Annie ceded nothing, using a steel spine to mask her mush for knees.

"Don't get too cocky, Flynn," she warned.

He held the remaining raspberry to her mouth, brushing it against her lower lip in a soft caress. At the same time his gaze locked with hers, lit with temptation and a humor she'd seen little of from the other men in her life. Damned if she didn't take the raspberry like a circus poodle performing for kibble.

"It's confidence, Annie, not cockiness."

He had her there. If confidence were a tradable commodity, Daniel Flynn would be a billionaire. And unless she picked up on this skill, she'd forever be broke.

Confidence, the best that she could figure, came from asserting power. And so long as she was in charge, she wanted to explore the power she held over Daniel Flynn. She would have kissed him, except she was too short to reach his mouth without his cooperation. Instead she tugged his black shirt free from his jeans. She slipped her hands beneath it and ran them across the warm skin of his stomach, feeling his abs tighten beneath her palms.

She smiled at his indrawn breath and the way he said her name as though it was a warning.

"Just testing a little," she said. "Do you bend, Daniel?" She followed the curve of his rib cage around to his back. Wow, but he felt good. Bummer she'd been acting like a trained poodle instead of a cat, because right about now she was ready to purr.

"Bend? I, erm…"

He trailed off as she drew her hands forward and slid the soft cotton shirt upward. His skin really was the delicious golden hue she half recalled from last night. He'd clearly seen the sun in more tropical locales than Ireland.

"You were saying?" she prompted, then with her eyes still meeting his, shimmied downward until she could sample what she'd exposed.

She kissed the spot right above the waistband of his jeans and laughed a little as he jumped beneath her mouth. She ventured upward and to the right a few inches, this time opening her mouth against him and nipping just enough to be certain she had his full attention. It occurred to her that she might have found the ideal food substitute for those stressful moments in life. She kissed him again, flicking her tongue against his skin.

His laughter sounded a little choked, which made her smile.

Daniel drew her upward, leaving her bereft of her favorite morning treat. "God, Annie, I'll bend like a pretzel if that's what you want."

Definitely in charge, she walked a circle around him, trailing her hand over his tight butt. "I'm still deciding what I want, but I'll add the pretzel thing to the list, okay?" she said when she was again in front of him. "And until then, I'll take a kiss."

"One within your rules, of course," he said, one dark brow raised.

She nodded in agreement. "Of course."

Daniel Flynn kissed as he did everything else she had seen him do—like a virtuoso. And though it generally wasn't her favorite state, Annie was okay with living in the moment. Stretching it out an hour or two didn't sound half-bad, either.

But since perfection never lasted long in her world, someone knocked at the suite's door. She could hear laughter and muffled voices from the other side.

"Damn," Daniel said, glancing toward the noise. "It must be Pat and God knows who else."

"Pat?"

He began tucking his shirt back into his jeans. "He was at dinner last night—the far end of the table," he replied in a distracted sort of way. "He'll be giving us a lift to the airport. I think he's forgotten that it's a crime for an Irishman to arrive early."

Pat and company knocked again, and someone called a laughing, "We know you're in there."

"Are you going to answer that?" Annie asked as she unclipped her still-damp hair and tried to tame its guy-induced disarray.

"In a minute," he said. "One promise from you, first. When we get back to Ann Arbor, no more icy Annie, if you could?"

She sighed. "Daniel, work is work."

"True, but the workday isn't twenty-four hours, especially since you've announced yourself a short-timer."

"I said that? I couldn't have."

"You did, and just a few minutes ago, too."

"You probably didn't hear me right," she blurted, moving into cover-your-ass mode.

"But I did."

"Let's talk about it later." She bolted to the door to admit Pat and his merry band of saviors. As Flynn shot her a dry look, Annie shuffled "Learn to panic with your mouth shut" to the top of her skills-to-be-acquired list.

And front and center on her reminder list—Irishmen *never* forget.

ON SATURDAY MORNING, Daniel sat with Hal in a dark, wood-paneled Hunt Club dining room. The place smacked of aristocracy in a way that made his refined-through-generations rebel blood go into high alarm. Of course, Annie's avoidance of him last night once they'd returned home might also have been enough to account for his current dark mood. He didn't expect her to bare her soul. Just a few bits of her body and a detail or two of her plans would suffice. Instead, here he was with Hal, who looked no happier than he, though undoubtedly for different reasons.

During coffee, they chatted about the places Daniel had taken Annie, and the possible recruits he'd talked to. When Daniel suggested that this conversation should include Annie, Hal brushed aside the thought.

"Annie will do what she's told," he replied. "The girl's like a granddaughter to me."

Daniel managed not to choke on his disbelief at the thought of Ms. Annie meekly following orders. He had thought his own family dysfunctional, but it seemed that they were bloody normal compared to some.

Breakfast was served, and Hal turned to his meal with enthusiasm. Between bites, he said, "I'll bet you're wondering why you're here."

Whether interpreted as "here in Ann Arbor" or "here

at breakfast," the response remained the same. "Yes, I'll admit to being a bit curious."

"Getting old is a bitch," Hal eventually said. He frowned at his plate and set aside his fork. "My arteries are blocked. Too much good food, I guess."

Daniel eyed the remains of sausages, potatoes and fried eggs in front of the man. "And you're on medication?"

"I was supposed to have surgery in May."

"Grand," he said, feeling grimmer than he had in months. Since a year ago April, to be exact, when he'd had to drag his da to Galway for prostate surgery. And this was the thanks fate threw him—another stubborn old bastard sure he could outlive the devil.

"I haven't keeled over, have I?" Hal pointed out before spearing a lone bite of sausage.

"Yet." Maybe this inability to admit to illness was a generational thing. Da had married late, and had his first son when he was already past forty. Hal was no younger than Da. Daniel hoped he wouldn't be nearly as thick when he reached seventy.

"So you were sitting in my family's pub instead of getting this taken care of?" Daniel asked.

"The trip was already booked." The older man at least had the sense to appear embarrassed as he offered up his excuse.

"If you're looking for me to applaud your foolishness, you've brought the wrong Flynn for the job."

"What I'm looking for is a voice of reason outside my family. I spent weeks in your pub, Daniel. I saw how you operated with your family. You're a born peacemaker."

"I've had a lifetime of experience with that lot. What am I to do here?"

Hal didn't answer directly. "I'm going to have an artery unplugged with a stent or some other damn thing put in, a week from Tuesday. You and Eva are the only two, other than my doctors, who know."

It shocked him none that Eva D'Onfrio knew, since he suspected that she'd been Hal's lover for decades. The rest did come as a surprise, though maybe not as much as it should. In the weeks that Hal had stayed in Clifden, he'd infrequently mentioned his sons.

"Why not tell your family?"

"The boys are already pushing for more responsibility. They'll be circling like wolves if they know I'm sick."

It was all Daniel could do not to remind Hal that the eldest of "the boys" was past fifty and likely well ready for more responsibility. Or early retirement.

"You underestimate them," he said instead.

"If anything, I overestimate them. But it's my own damn fault. They are what I made them."

To live the life of a kingmaker… "What do you want me to do for you, Hal?"

"Come to the hospital."

He nodded. "Of course."

"And not a word to anyone until this is done. I need your promise."

This was harder to give, for it didn't take a seer to know that sooner or later he'd be putting himself in a bad way with Annie. Yet Hal's privacy was his own, and despite his frustration, Daniel counted the man among his friends.

"You have my word," he finally said, knowing that in exchange he'd eventually suffer death by ice from Ms. Annie. It shouldn't matter. He'd be moving on, after all, and in a matter of months she'd be no more than a memory. The thought sent a cold spear through Daniel's heart.

"Thank you," Hal replied. "You won't be sorry."

But he already was.

11

On Monday, the seventh floor, where Annie's office was located, was in battle mode. The secretarial pool and corporate drones sat stone-faced at their cubicles. Those employees lucky enough to have doors to their offices had shut them. The galley was a wasteland, with an open box of chocolate chip cookies languishing uneaten on the counter. Annie rescued one, then moved on.

As she walked down the corridor, tension knotted tighter under her skin. Headquarters had always been a loud place, taking its cue from Hal's personality. This tomblike atmosphere was unnatural. Whatever was going on would have to wait, though. Annie had another unnatural silence to address.

Sasha was proving harder to raise than the ghost of her black sheep uncle Rob, and Annie was getting desperate. It totally sucked to have experienced an event as wild as her travels with Flynn, and not be able to dissect it with Sasha. Annie knew she needed someone to talk some sense into her, or better yet, tell her that it was okay to indulge in the mad, mindless fling she'd been considering as she lay in her cool and empty bed the past three nights. Sasha was the girl for the job.

Yesterday, Annie had even considered camping outside her house, except she had laundry to do, food to buy, a zillion e-mails to answer and hours of research to finish on restaurant design groups. Besides, she knew she could corner Sasha this morning.

Annie knocked on her friend's door. Before she even had time to respond, Rachel, Evil Queen of Marketing, strolled up and said, "Sick day."

"Is it anything serious?" Annie asked, then immediately realized she'd committed a tactical error. Her one consistent defense against Rachel's venom was being more in-the-know.

Rachel's mouth edged from its usual flat-line mode to a smug curve. "You're asking me? What, there's trouble in paradise?"

"Other than the standard annoying reptile, no," she replied.

Rachel turned heel on her faux-lizard pumps and stalked off, but not without first issuing her obligatory hiss.

Giving up on Sasha for the time being, Annie inventoried the cubicles for someone who might be willing to talk, but came up empty. Among the downsides of being so firmly linked with Hal Donovan was the fact that most people assumed she was a snitch. Not that anyone had the nerve to say it to her face.

Annie returned unhappy and uninformed to her office. Waiting on the desk were glossy presentation materials from a few of the designers she'd contacted prior to her forced march across the USA. Beneath them she found new copies of trade magazines from the franchise associations she'd joined.

Annie pushed aside the magazines as dead—or at least dead-for-now—issues and dialed into her voice mail. She had three messages from her sister, whom she'd apparently forgotten to tell she was leaving town—or that she'd returned.

She phoned Elizabeth and assured her that she'd neither been kidnapped nor drowned in the bathtub. Luckily, Elizabeth was in her work mode, which meant that there was precious little time to spare for sisterly lecturing.

"I've heard back from Paul Housden," Elizabeth said.

"Who?"

"My corporate recruiting contact in New York. He wants you to forward your résumé. If he likes what he sees, he'll meet with you."

"In New York?" Annie couldn't quite fight down the panic. She'd barely recovered from the flight home. Daniel had once again held her hand and done all those wonderful Flynn-like things, but that didn't make her especially excited to repeat the experience on her own.

Lectures were in short supply, but Lizzie still had time to sound annoyed. "Yes, in New York. That *is* where you want to be, right?"

Annie's answer was automatic. "Of course."

"I made the contact. Knock yourself out and do the follow-up."

Annie dug in her desk drawer for a pen, then flipped over the first available sheet of paper. "Give me his number."

Elizabeth reeled out number, company name and address. Annie frantically scribbled, then repeated it back to her. When she hung up, she found Daniel Flynn standing in her doorway. Pleasure at the sight of him warred with alarm over what he might have heard.

"Been there long?"

"Not so very," he said, giving nothing up in his expression. "Mind if I step inside?"

She flipped over the information she'd just written, then said, "Come on in."

He was dressed for business today, not in a suit, but in freshly pressed khakis and an olive-colored sweater that looked like fine woven silk. Annie folded one hand over the other, hoping that would quell her urge to reach out and touch. He settled in one of the two guest chairs opposite her desk.

"Did you have a fine weekend?" he asked.

"It was a game of catch up."

"It must have been brutal, what with you not having the time to return even one of my calls."

"Sorry. I was really busy," she said, which sounded a whole lot more mature than "I needed to hash out the pros and cons of sleeping with you."

And since the matter remained unhashed, seeing him again was messing with her already scrambled sense of order.

"I've furniture now, and a full fridge," he said. "And some hope of surviving till August."

"That's great." Maybe she didn't want wild sex with him—or maybe she did—but she definitely didn't want to think about Flynn leaving. She nudged the mouse of her computer and brought up the time line she'd made for the pub. "I have two chefs coming in this afternoon to talk about menu. Are you free?"

"I'll have to check."

Check what? she wanted to ask. She blew past a couple of lesser design candidates she'd felt compelled to see for form's sake and focused on the following week's schedule. "We also have the Ars/Ullman design team coming in next Tuesday. You should probably be there."

"Tuesday? I won't be able to make it."

"Nothing you need to check to know that one?"

"Not a thing. Any possibility of moving the meeting to Wednesday?"

Could the guy never simply follow? "Nope."

"Then go on without me."

"What's up on Tuesday?"

"A prior obligation."

"Work?"

He glanced out the window, then back at her. "In a sense."

"Ah." Tricky, setting one foot outside the domain where she was allowed to pry. As she considered her next step, she rolled her mouse back and forth across its pad. Daniel's expression bordered on wary as he watched her. That, she supposed, was some consolation.

"It's no loss, going forward without me," he eventually said. "My idea of good design is sufficient seats at the bar."

"No problem. I was only asking because I should. I can handle it myself." Her words were the truth as far as they went. What she couldn't handle was her unhealthy level of curiosity over his alternate plans.

Annie quit torturing her computer's mouse. She wanted to deal with Daniel in the same direct manner with which she'd flattened Garth's toes. Wanted to, but somehow couldn't. Maybe it was because she didn't want to risk the feeling that something really cool had begun to happen between them. Or maybe she was just a victim of the blanket of doom that hovered outside her office door. Either way, she found herself playing coy—and coy really put a knot in her stomach.

"Annie, what's bothering you?"

"Nothing," she lied, then pinned on a more cheerful expression. "You know, I spent the weekend looking for the missing connection and just couldn't nail it. What was the link between all the places we went last week?"

He smiled. "You could have ended your suffering by picking up your phone and talking to me."

"Humor me now."

Daniel shrugged. "It's basic stuff, really. It was the welcome. At each place there was a sense of community...of truly belonging."

Belonging. The word nearly knocked the breath from her, and not because she cared in more than a vague get-past-this-mess sort of way about Hal's pub dream. No, this was a sudden, personal, to-the-gut blow. *When had she started feeling as if she no longer belonged?*

"That's the key to what Hal wants," Daniel was saying. "What you need to deliver."

How the hell had this slipped by her?

She realized she must have let at least part of her question escape aloud when Flynn laughed. "How? Magic, alchemy...I haven't a clue. If I did, I'd be a billionaire. In Ireland, the welcome's simple. It's not such as easy a task in a country as diverse as yours."

He stretched his long legs out before him and leaned back into the chair. "And as long as we're asking questions, here's one I've been waiting since Friday to ask you. In Seattle, you called yourself a short-timer. What did you mean by that?"

Annie was the one to look away this time, mostly to

see if anyone was in earshot. Just to be safe, she walked to her door and closed it.

"Nothing concrete," she said after she'd turned back to Daniel. "I've just been playing with the idea of relocating."

"And have you anyplace in mind?" he asked.

"New York."

He smiled, but there didn't seem to be a whole lot of happy backing it up. "Ah, the overflow room for hell."

"Funny, Flynn."

"And true, too."

Annie was about to rebut this piece of insanity when her phone rang. She quickly covered the five steps back to her desk and lifted the receiver, hoping it was Sasha. Instead, Mrs. D. was on the other end, wanting to know if Annie had seen Daniel.

"He's right in front of me," Annie replied, frowning as she caught him reading the papers on her desk. She edged between him and his snooping range.

"Then ask him to tell you that everyone's waiting for the two of you in the boardroom," Mrs. D. said.

Saving her annoyance for its proper target, Annie gave Mrs. D. a quick thanks, then hung up. While she grabbed a notepad and a pen, she asked Daniel, "Any reason in particular you didn't tell me that we've got a roomful of people waiting for us?"

He rose from his chair. "You owed me a chat."

"Yeah, and someone owes me about three weeks of vacation on a tropical beach with a fifth of rum, but that has to wait, too."

"Not too long, I'm hoping," he said. "I'm finding I'm not as good at waiting as I once was."

Annie paused. "What's that supposed to mean?"

"Just this." He came to her and unclipped her hair from the workday knot she'd twisted it into.

Using her free hand, she tried to shoo him away. "Don't mess with my hair."

"It's so beautiful down," he said as he combed his long fingers through it. "Now relax. The Donovan boys can sit and contemplate the reach of their empire for a few minutes longer, but I need to do this."

His kiss was slow, full, rich—and dangerous in the extreme to a woman who'd just begun to think about what it means to belong. She allowed herself to enjoy him for about five seconds, then found the willpower to step away.

Daniel handed her the clip he'd slid from her hair. Annie tossed it onto her desk, then did her best to straighten up and look unkissed.

"You bend beautifully, love," he said just before she opened the door to her office.

To Annie, it was feeling a whole lot more as though she was about to snap.

WHEN ANNIE AND DANIEL stepped off the elevator on the top floor, it seemed to her that the headquarters' tension level had increased with the altitude. Even the unflappable Mrs. D. appeared harried. Her usually sleek silver pageboy looked frizzy, as though it had flirted with an overheated blow-dryer, and her expression was equally heated.

"You'd better go on in," she said, motioning toward the boardroom door.

"And I wish you luck," Annie thought she heard the woman say just as she and Daniel cleared the double doors to the room. Inside, Hal and his four sons sat on opposing sides of the enormous oblong rosewood table.

"Sorry we're late," Daniel said as he slipped into a chair at Hal's right hand—the one where Annie normally sat. "My fault entirely."

Of course Hal's sons still chose to glare at Annie as she took up a compromise position to Daniel's right.

"Can we get this moving?" Duane, Donovan's General Counsel and son number three, asked while glancing at his watch.

"What's the matter, are we cutting too close to a tee time?" asked Richard, the eldest surviving son after Miami Rob.

Annie had never figured out how a man so wed to Brooks Brothers clothes and a holier-than-thou attitude had managed to father Sasha. And only because he was Sasha's dad could Annie tolerate him at all.

Sons two and four riffled through their papers like the number crunchers they were.

Annie glanced over at Daniel, who intently watched the scene. She'd lived in the middle of the infighting for so long that she generally tuned it out.

"All right, just to spare myself some aggravation, let's get going," Hal said. He glanced down at a sheet of paper in front of him. "First on the list, I want to shut down the State Street location for renovations effective June twenty-fifth. Howard," he directed son number four, "tell the regional manager to offer the staff temporary jobs in the Lansing and Royal Oak locations."

Howard looked nearly as shocked as Annie felt. Her stomach began to fight the chocolate chip cookie she'd eaten earlier. She'd assumed that despite all of his "need to know" puffing days earlier, Hal had actually already given the details of his plan to his sons. Considering the family track record, that assumption pretty much proved the old "assume=ass out of you and me" formula. She slumped lower in her chair, trying to keep out of the line of fire.

"I agree the place is in need of updating, but why not just have the contractors work after-hours?" Howard asked his father. He could be a little slow on the uptake, so she was relieved that he'd pegged the problem on the first try.

"Won't do," Hal said, rolling his fat pen between his fingers as though it was a cigar. "This will be a total revamp. I'm figuring it will be down for six weeks."

The statement gained Richard's attention. He leaned forward, steepling his perfectly manicured hands in front of him. "What do you mean, revamp?"

"We're going from pizza to a pub," Hal said. "It's the first location for the new chain."

"Let me see if I have this. Just to amuse yourself, you're going to close our most profitable location in the state and keep it shut down right through Art Fair?"

Each July, Ann Arbor hosted two massive, juried outdoor art fairs. Restaurants in the area couldn't turn out food fast enough during that week.

"It doesn't matter if you 'have it,' Richie," Hal said. "It's a done deal and you don't need to bother with it."

"How about the fact that our same-store numbers are down from last year, utility costs are up thirty percent and we're bleeding money from workers' comp claims? Should I bother with those, Dad?"

Annie watched as Hal's usual hypertensive flush grew even more crimson. His eldest son was almost a matching hue. It was a modern-day duel—heart attacks at thirty paces. Annie might not be crazy about Richard, but outside of one or two recurring evil fantasies, she didn't want to see him keel over.

"End of discussion," Hal said. He glanced at the list on the table in front of him. "Next up is chain performance in Northern California. Duane—"

"We're not done with State Street," Richard cut in.

"Duane," Hal repeated through clenched teeth, "I want—"

Looking none too thrilled, Duane took on the role of peacekeeper. "Richard, maybe we should—"

Richard's eyes narrowed. "Shut up."

"*You* shut up," Hal snapped. "I'm in charge here. I grew this place from nothing."

Annie pondered how long it would take her to talk her doctor into a ninety-day scrip for antianxiety meds.

"And made each pizza yourself for the first three years… We've all heard the speech enough to give it ourselves," Richard said. "And this time, Dad, you're doing the listening. The old days are dead. You can't keep running this business like a corner shop. I don't know if it's age, or if you're just not interested anymore, but the details are getting away from you. You're slipping."

Daniel pushed back his chair. "Perhaps I should be leaving the room."

Annie also moved marginally, figuring she'd make good on an escape when he did.

"Stay," Hal ordered at the same time as Richard was saying "go."

Daniel looked to Hal and nodded his consent. "I'll stay then."

Damn. Annie settled in.

"I'm slipping, am I?"

Richard's answer was a flat yes.

"In what way?"

"This pub idea, signing him on to do who the hell knows what," he said with a jab of an index finger in Daniel's direction. "Promoting Ms. Rutherford over other more qualified candidates time and again when she's done nothing that any first-year MBA grad couldn't have done, and—"

Hal's hand hit the table with enough force that even his three others sons, who'd been as still as stone, jumped.

"Enough! This is my business and if I decide to give the whole thing away or close down tomorrow, you get no vote."

Richard stood. "Don't be so sure." The conference room door slammed behind him.

Annie focused on her hands, folded on the table in front of her. Yup, those knuckles shone stress-white. And she couldn't count fast enough to measure her pulse.

"Do you three have anything to add?" Hal asked his other sons.

They made bland noises in the negative.

"If you're not going to stand with me on this, you might as well follow your brother."

They proclaimed fealty, but Annie noted the way their gazes kept drifting to the door that Richard had exited.

So this was how empires crumbled...

Annie's job hunt had just moved from a "should do" to a "do it at the speed of light."

12

BLOODY SHEEP-REEKING hell. Daniel's family fought, but beneath the words remained love. And the Donovans? If there was love—or even remote affection—it had been so deeply buried in resentment that an archaeologist would be hard-pressed to unearth it.

The elevator chimed its arrival, pulling Daniel from his black thoughts. He and Annie stepped inside. She pushed the button for the seventh floor, then moved to the back. Her face was a study in tension, jaw set and eyes looking nearly bruised.

On impulse, Daniel reached out and tapped the ground floor button. Her brows rose marginally, but she said nothing. The elevator slowed, then stopped at seven. Annie took a step forward. Daniel hooked his hand around her wrist, permitting her to go no farther.

"What are you doing?"

"Abducting you," he said while reaching to hit the close doors button with his free hand. "And it's for your own good, too."

"Flynn…"

"Trust me," he said as the doors slipped shut and the elevator descended again. When they exited at the ground floor, it was all Daniel could do not to give the mural of Hal and his sons a rude salute before walking past it.

He'd wager that not one of the Donovan clan had ever smiled as beneficently as they did in that godlike portrait. And he especially damned Richard for having spoken ill of Annie in front of her. The man had been not only unbusinesslike, but cruel.

"Let's find some sunshine," he said to Annie as he ushered her toward the door.

She proved unwilling. "You can't always walk away from trouble."

"No, sometimes you can run, though those shoes of yours might make it a risk." He'd noted with approval the change to her wardrobe since their days in Chicago. Her shoes were, to be honest, damn sexy, with narrow high heels and open in front so that her crimson-painted toenails enticed him.

"Hey, I like my shoes," Annie said.

"Actually, so do I."

She almost smiled. "Thanks, but they're not the point, anyway. I meant what I said on a metaphorical level."

"Grand. So long as I promise to bring you back, can we really walk now?"

He watched as she looked through the plate glass to the bright world beyond. "Twenty minutes, no more."

Daniel took what crumbs she'd handed him. They headed south on Main Street, walking elbow to elbow. He'd have liked to have taken her hand, but knew Annie would never allow it. That he'd persuaded a kiss from her while in the privacy of her office had been a full-blown miracle.

They were nearing a coffee place when Annie said, "Hang on. I've earned a treat."

Inside, she ordered a frozen mocha drink topped

with a fat pillow of whipped cream and chocolate shavings. Daniel patted his back pocket, now days and days empty of cigarettes. He had most definitely earned a smoke, but knew that Annie would have his hide should he suggest they stop for a pack. In America, some vices were better received than others.

"They're not always so bad, you know," Annie said once they'd continued their walk.

She referred, without doubt, to the Donovans.

"And I'd expect that sometimes they're even worse," he replied.

She laughed. "True, but really only in the last month or so, otherwise I would have left a long time ago. Still, I'm sure, right about now, you're relieved that you're only here until August."

Daniel smiled in answer. Truth was, this afternoon he planned to check availability of return flights for just after Hal's hospital visit. He could no more keep peace in the Donovan family than he could survive in Annie's dubious paradise of Manhattan. The best he could do was live up to his promises, then put an ocean between himself and the Donovan clan. The greatest price to be paid was losing the additional time with Annie, but their fate had always been inevitable.

"So what will you do about this pub chain of Hal's?" he asked, thinking of how her life would move on without him.

Annie sighed. "My game plan, lame as it is, is to keep out of the battle and pretend that it's all going to work out. I'll get State Street up and running, and lie through my teeth to anyone who asks how it's going." She slowed her busy-woman pace and looked up at him. "You know, if someone had told me a week ago that I'd be saying this, I'd have told them they were insane, but I'm glad you're here. Thank you."

He doubted she'd be quite as grateful had she any idea the direction his thoughts were running. "It's been my pleasure."

PLEASURE... WALKING WITH Flynn brought Annie pleasure. A caffeine-laden iced mocha wasn't too shabby, either. Her job, however, was turning into a veritable pleasure-suck.

Granted, she knew she'd never exactly been Richard's Employee of the Month, but he'd never skewered her in the middle of a meeting before, either. She'd accomplished a lot for the Donovans, dammit. She was the only reason they'd surfed the demographics wave and had pizza carry-outs up and running on the new edges of urban sprawl. She'd dealt with Hal better than any of them, and she'd been loyal, turning down offers to go with competing companies. Maybe none of this qualified her for sainthood, but it definitely justified her existence. So who did Richard think should have been promoted above her?

Annie knew he wasn't referring to Sasha. To the extent he considered his daughter at all, he seemed to view her as a decoration. He had no perceivable favorites among his employees in the finance department. Okay, so that was mystery number one.

Mystery number two—the question of why she should care about mystery number one if she was so set on leaving—was more easily solved. Annie's pride was smarting, as was her confidence.

Frustrated with her pace, Annie darted around two women who were slowing to look in the window of a gallery. Yeah, nice deal. What did someone do for a living that they could window-shop on a Monday morning? She wanted *that* job.

"Off and to the races?" Daniel called to her.

She waited for him to catch up. "Sorry. Maybe we should just go back." Emotionally, it was like running though knee-high mud, dragging the warring Donovans with her.

While they waited at the corner for the light to change, Daniel tipped her face upward. "Still ten minutes short of happy, I'd say."

A gross underestimate, if ever she'd heard one. Still, she knew what would nudge her down the road to happy.

"Are you free for dinner tonight?" she asked.

He shook his head. "Sorry, I'd sort of promised to meet up with the ladies I met at market when I came to town."

It was tough to be jealous of women in their seventies, but Annie was up for the challenge. "Oh, okay. No big deal."

"How about some time later this evening? I could ring you when I'm back home."

"Don't worry about it. It was just a thought." She had the feeling that by the time Daniel called, she'd be in the bathtub, anyway. Bad workdays often led to long soaks with stacks of reading material and a fat chocolate bar at her fingertips.

Annie pushed through the front door to headquarters and shivered at the chill in the air. Daniel and she both exited the elevator at the seventh floor, he to the office she'd made sure was waiting for him this week, and she to her own.

Once there, Annie ignored anything resembling work and focused on her résumé. Yes, she knew this was a weasel-like use of Donovan time, but it was pay-back hour. Or at least payback forty-five minutes. Content with her rough draft, she zipped it off via e-mail to Elizabeth for review, figuratively thumbing her nose at the corporate computer godfather who was no doubt recording her transgression and forwarding it for inclusion in her personnel file.

That done, she called Sasha for the four hundred thirty-seventh damn time, but this time actually got an answer.

"No, I'm not speaking to you," Sasha said when she picked up the phone.

Where would civilization be without caller ID.?

"Well, technically you *are* speaking to me," Annie pointed out.

"But only to tell you that I'm not, which has to fall into a loophole."

"So do you hate me?"

Annie waited out the silence until Sasha said, "I haven't quite decided yet."

"How about if I take you out for Mexican food tonight and do a groveling belly crawl through the restaurant? Think that will tip the scales in my favor?"

"It couldn't hurt," her friend conceded. "So you'll be buying margaritas, too?"

"Of course."

"Ah, the full suck-up, then."

Annie smiled. "Only the best for you, babe."

"Armando's at eight," Sasha said. "And bring lots of money."

As she hung up, Annie felt some of the weight of the morning lifting. Work stank, but maybe she was on the road to getting her best friend back.

DANIEL SURVEYED the small office he'd been allotted down the hallway from Ms. Annie. He really didn't have much to do today, other than the chefs' interviews after lunch. He supposed he could write, but this space was like a deprivation chamber—no art, bland desk, blander view of the neighboring building. He required a bit more in the way of life around him to get his brain rolling.

He checked his watch. It would be nearing four in the afternoon back home, a relatively quiet time at the pub. He lifted the phone and dialed.

"Flynn's," his brother Seán said. His voice was so clear and familiar that it seemed impossible they were thousands of miles apart.

"It's Daniel, Seán. Is Da there?"

"Nah, he's off driving Mam mad today."

"He's not working?" Da was guaranteed to be behind the bar every afternoon when his friends came in for a pint and talk of whether Galway would best Limerick in hurling that season.

"He's threatening to retire, which has Mam muttering about talking a job in the office at Abbeyglen Hotel just so she won't have him underfoot all day."

"Da's feeling well, isn't he?"

"Good as ever," Seán said. "Except he won't even talk about James. And before you ask, yes, Jamie's still in Salthill. He says he won't be coming back until Da apologizes."

Daniel had no idea what had spurred the latest spat, and it really didn't matter. "He'll apologize when we have a year without rain."

Seán snorted. "Likely not even then."

From the other end of the line came a muffled

sound, almost as though his brother were juggling the phone.

"What are you doing?" Daniel asked.

"Playing darts, of course."

He should have known. Years ago, while still at university, Daniel had taken a summer job in a London pub. Other than a hangover that lasted until the next term's end, the other thing he'd brought home with him was a dartboard and an addiction to the game. His original board still hung in the family pub, along with two more to keep Flynn's guests content.

When business was slow, all the Flynn brothers had taken to playing what was fairly much extreme darts, shooting from behind the bar counter to the board at the far wall. The game drove their da mad, and had scared religion into more than one hapless customer who'd stepped into the pub at the wrong instant.

"And so who's working the bar besides you?" he asked, trying to gauge just how guilty he should feel for not being there.

"Aislinn's been helping out, but the only drink she knows is beer, and she's a terror at counting change." Seán paused in what Daniel knew was a moment of dart-throwing concentration, then said, "You wouldn't be knowing her favorite kind of flowers, would you?"

"Wild roses," he said. "None of the boxed ones, but from the roadside."

"Figures she'd make me work," his brother muttered.

Daniel smiled. He couldn't begrudge either Seán or Aislinn their happiness. "I take it you've found some attributes to make up for her lack of bar skills."

"One or two, though her hatchet tongue's not among

them." Another pause from his brother and another dart thrown. "Double bull!" Seán crowed.

"More like bullshit, I'd be guessing," Daniel replied.

"Don't be taking it so hard. You can't remain champion forever."

Not without his board, he couldn't.

"Do me a favor," Daniel said. "Package up my board and ship it to me by courier."

"And what will you do for me?"

"Pretend I believe you just made that shot."

"Fair enough," his brother replied.

After he hung up, Daniel felt pleased enough to pull out his laptop and begin to write. A dartboard wasn't much to anchor happiness to, but it seemed that it was enough for now.

ANNIE STAYED AT WORK until almost eight, seeing no point in heading home before meeting Sasha. It wasn't as though she had to get all prettied up to do her belly crawl of shame.

The spots that Donovan's leased in the city parking structure for its more senior employees were nearly empty when Annie hurried through. She noted that both Hal's and Richard's cars were still there. She hoped, for their sake as well as her sanity, that the two were conducting truce negotiations.

Annie pushed the door unlock button on her key chain as she approached her car. Parked to her left was Evil Queen Rachel's silver Audi TT Coupe. Annie had dreamt of owning one herself, until Rachel had gotten there first.

As Annie approached, she noted that Rachel was in the little car, and that she wasn't alone. If it had been any day but this, one which was in dire need of amusement, Annie would have done the polite thing and looked away. Instead she slowed, trying to see if she recognized the car's male occupant—no easy feat when Rachel was sucking his face. Clearly, there was no need to worry about disturbing this couple's clinch.

Annie opened her door and slid into the car. Before closing her door, she took advantage of her improved viewing perspective. Make that improved, disgusting and very educational.

If she were Dorothy with magical ruby slippers, she'd be clicking her heels for all she was worth and giving it a heartfelt, "There's no place like Manhattan. There's no place like Manhattan." But she was Annie with nonmagical though admittedly pretty cool shoes, and so she was stuck next to a whole lot of ugly.

She had sat through countless meetings wondering how Richard Donovan could be so into wardrobe and yet keep his ridiculous comb-over hairstyle. Now she knew the answer—it was so Rachel could make that flap of black hair stand upright as she ran her fingers through it. Annie was also now pretty clear on who Richard felt should be promoted over her, and what it took to get there…thanks, but no thanks.

She figured she could exit politely or do it with a bang. Option number two won. Annie slammed her car door hard enough to make the sound ricochet like a gunshot off the concrete of the structure. When Richard and Rachel untwined and looked her way, she waggled her fingers in a cheery goodbye, then took off.

On the way to Armando's, Annie engaged in a should-I-tell-Sasha-or-should-I-not debate. It wasn't as though this would mean the end of a marriage—Sasha's mom had wisely divorced Richard years ago, just as her grandmom had divorced Hal. Still, what good would it do Sasha if she knew? None that Annie could perceive.

As she was pulling into the tiny lot behind the restaurant, Annie finally settled on keeping the garage grope to herself. Of course the question remained whether she was coordinated enough to tiptoe around two topics—her résumé polishing and Richard's poor taste—in the same meal. She had to admit that the odds weren't good.

After a brief hunt, Annie found Sasha in a booth near the back of the always crowded restaurant.

"Should I begin groveling?" she asked as she approached the table.

Despite her claimed sick day, Sasha looked as gorgeous as usual. "Nah," she said. "Just don't eat all the salsa and chips and we'll be square."

"I think I'd rather grovel." Despite her statement, Annie slid into her side of the booth and thanked Sasha as her friend poured her a margarita from a pitcher already on the table.

After a sip, Annie got down to business. "I feel rotten. I'm so sorry for not noticing how unhappy you've been about your job."

"Don't sweat it. It's not like anyone else has noticed, either. Life as the Invisible Donovan can be a grind."

Annie laughed. "Invisible? Not quite."

Sasha shrugged. "I am in all the ways that matter. No one ever asks for my input. I think it's mostly because Dad and Grandpa are afraid I'm as irresponsible as my uncle Rob. Not that I can blame them much, given my record."

Since it was tough to refute the accuracy of Sasha's assessment, Annie remained silent.

"So," Sasha said, "here's my plan... I've signed up for one of those test review courses, then I'm going to take the GRE." Annie must have looked as lost as she felt because Sasha added, "You know, the Graduate Record Exam."

"Yeah, I knew that, but what are you planning to do?"

"I've decided to get my master's in social work."

This conversation was a case of serial déjà vu. "Um...okay. Sure."

"Annie, I mean it. This isn't like the time I went to culinary school or my shot at a philosophy degree. I'm serious about this."

"Do you even have your bachelor's degree?"

"Of course I do."

Annie frowned. "I don't remember a graduation party."

"No one's very festive when you take seven years to graduate, okay?" Sasha said after dipping a chip into her margarita, then chowing it.

"Good point."

"I need a change. I want a job where I feel like I'm making a difference in someone's life." She laughed. "Actually, at this point I'd settle for a job where they just notice whether I show up."

"So you're going to leave Donovan's..."

"Not right away. I'm going to ask for a part-time schedule that will fit around my classes."

"It sounds like a great plan."

Sasha smiled. "Do you really think so? You've always had your head on so straight about career stuff that I figured if this idea got past you, it had to be good."

Okay, this was the moment when Annie admitted

that she was a total fraud, that she had no idea what she wanted to do and that she wished she could come up with a career goal half as solid as Sasha's. Of course, that would totally wipe out Sasha's growing happiness over her big change.

Annie made some inane, perky comment, opened the menu and contemplated ordering one of everything just to keep her mouth shut. Friendship could be a calorie-laden thing.

IT WAS CREEPING UP on eleven when Annie pulled onto Cobblestone Court. Instead of heading straight home, she drove past Daniel's town house. Lights still shone inside, drawing her. She looped to the end of the block, then slowly drove back.

Near the end of her dinner with Sasha, she'd finally broached the subject of a fling with Daniel. Instead of getting the Sasha stamp of approval, she had shot down the idea.

"Annie, you're incapable of a real fling. You get too attached," she'd said. "I mean, look at the collections of stuff in your condo. You can't keep Daniel Flynn. He'll leave, and you'll be a mess."

Sasha was right. Annie couldn't even count Garth as a fling. Worse yet, she hadn't liked him enough for their relationship to even qualify as buddy sex. She'd talked herself into being attracted to him out of convenience. The guy had fit into her schedule.

So was Daniel Flynn convenient? Annie seriously doubted it. His arrival hadn't been easy and his departure would no doubt spawn an eating binge sufficient to sweep clean the cookie shelves at the corner market. Yes, she'd become attached to him. What other reason could she possibly have for sleeping with a Space Needle salt-and-pepper set on her nightstand?

Annie sighed. Life would be so easy if she were, well, just a little easier herself.

She stopped just above his driveway. If she had any willpower, she'd keep going. But since she and willpower weren't even passing acquaintances, she parked in front of his garage and walked up the steps. Daniel came to the door only seconds after she rang the bell.

He was barefoot, wearing jeans and an old T-shirt from a bar in Munich. He looked scruffy, disreputable and still the hottest guy she'd ever seen.

"Hi," she said.

His smile grew. "Hi."

"I'm not bothering you, am I?" she asked over the pounding of her heart.

"Never." He glanced over his shoulder. "I was just writing a bit. I've an outline due to my publisher, but it's not as though they're expecting it tonight."

"I could always…" She finished the offer that she hoped he wouldn't take by gesturing at the darkness behind her.

"Come in, love."

As she stepped over the threshold, the sense of ease Annie had been chasing all day finally came to her. She felt at home.

13

"MUCH TO MY REGRET, I'm not here for sex," Annie announced as she stepped inside. "And I'm not feeling especially witty, wise or beautiful tonight, either." She hesitated and then added, "Okay…maybe just a little beautiful."

Daniel considered himself no expert when it came to the female mind. After years of dealing first with his mam and then his girlfriends, he was, however, skilled at treading carefully.

"Should I ask what you are besides beautiful, then?"

"Tired. Missing you. In need of a hug."

And he felt in need of holding her. Daniel drew Annie into his arms. His heart seemed to grow warmer, easier, as she nearly melted into him.

"This feels so good," she murmured, her head against his chest. "Maybe we could just stay here all night."

As his sole pieces of rental furniture were a bedroom set and a kitchen table, the idea had some merit. Despite her words, though, Annie too soon drew away. She walked into his empty living room.

"Love what you've done with the place," she said, wrinkling her nose. "We're definitely the yin and yang of home décor."

"I've a kitchen table, if that's any help."

She sighed. "What I want is one of those overstuffed recliners. You know, where you pull the lever, your feet fly to the ceiling and you're stuck until someone comes along to haul you out?"

He laughed. "I saw a few in the rental catalog, but managed to resist."

"You don't know what you're missing, Flynn. So are you still sleeping on the floor?" she asked as she wandered toward the bedroom.

He knew a moment's thanks that he'd picked up his dirty clothes, if not made his bed.

"Guess not," she said, raising her brows at his king-size bed. She tested the mattress with her hands. "Firm, just the way I like it. Do you mind if I..."

"Not at all."

She slipped off her shoes. "Don't get the wrong idea. This is all about comfort. You stay on your side, and I'll stay on mine, okay?"

Daniel knew it was as good as he'd be getting tonight, so he stretched out and watched as Ms. Annie settled in.

"It's been one of those days, you know?" she said.

"It has," he agreed.

They lay in companionable silence. It came as a total gobsmack to Daniel to realize that while he'd like to poach on Annie's side of the bed and see about bending her rules a bit, he was happy—for the moment, at least—just being with her.

"All the craziness at work got me thinking tonight," she eventually said. "We need to talk about this note you want from me."

"We do?"

She rolled onto her side, facing him, and propped her head on her left hand. "How much longer are you going to be in town?"

He wasn't sure what bearing this had on lovemaking, but he was willing to explore the connection.

"Seven weeks, more or less." Definitely less, if he considered the time he'd be devoting to Hal and his hospital issue next week.

"And do you think we'll ever see each other again once you've left?"

The hungry, prowling part of him wanted to lie, but Annie deserved better. "With you wanting Manhattan and me wandering about, it's unlikely, isn't it?"

She nodded. "Here's the problem...I'm not good at letting go of things I care about, Daniel. Clocks, salt shakers, jobs...and especially people. And I care about you. *Really* care about you. As it is, I keep thinking about what it's going to be like after you leave. Will you call or e-mail? Should I send you a Christmas card?"

"Annie, it's possible that you've been thinking too hard about all of this."

"No, I'm thinking just hard enough." She resettled and gazed up at the ceiling for a few moments. "Some women are good at grabbing happiness...stronger women than I am right now."

Violating the boundary between them, he reached out to smooth a wild lock of her hair. She relaxed under his touch and her eyes slipped closed. He wondered if she could feel how much he cared for her, how much he wanted to see her happy.

"Give me the time to work on my confidence, okay?" she said. "Once I'm sure I have this witty and wise thing down—and I'm getting close—it'll be a lot easier for me to step into something I know is guaranteed to end."

Much to his regret, Annie was already a wise, wise woman, and Daniel was damned to be a gentleman.

AN AMERICAN HOSPITAL smelled much the same as an Irish one—unpleasant. Perhaps this wasn't the sharpest observation that Daniel had ever made, but it wasn't bad for one made not much past dawn. He sat with Hal in a cardiac catheterization lab's waiting room nearly fifty minutes' drive from Ann Arbor.

"Don't you think you're carrying this secrecy a bit far?" he asked Hal. "It's not as though the U of M Hospital couldn't have swallowed you without anyone noticing."

Hal set aside the anglers' magazine he'd been pretending to read. "It had to be here. Back home, Richard would have found out, and he's a damn rottweiler. Now that he's sunk his teeth into the idea of forcing me out of the CEO's chair, he'll never let go."

Daniel took a sip of coffee to hide his smile over the deranged Donovan dynamics. Hal had sounded nearly proud of his son, who had made no secret of his consultations with lawyers over the past week.

"And have you made excuses for your absence?" Daniel asked.

Hal waved the magazine he'd brought along. "I'm at a private fishing lodge in northern Ontario. Rumor has it I'm having a hell of a good time."

Daniel smiled. "Grand. Now what are the rest of your plans?"

"The cardiologist says I should be released tomorrow morning. You'll take me back to the office, and—"

"I'll be taking you straight home."

The older man set his jaw at a bulldog angle. "Then Eva will take me back to the office."

Daniel laughed. "Right. We both know she'll have you home, wrapped in a blanket and coddled to death."

Hal responded with a grumpy "huh," then glanced up at the desk where a clerk was flipping through files, preparing to call another group of patients.

"I should be going back there soon," he said. "I lied to Eva and told her that I wasn't scheduled until eleven...didn't want her fussing over me."

"My point exactly."

"Well, see if you can calm her down by the time I'm in recovery."

"Eric Nagel," the clerk called. "Roberta Tokarski...Hal Donovan."

Hal stood. "Guess my number's up," he said in what Daniel recognized as gallows humor.

Daniel rose, feeling bloody insufficient in the role of Hal's family. He wanted to give the man comfort, but the best he could summon was a handshake and a hearty, "You'll do fine."

Hal looked over his shoulder once before walking with the others through a set of double doors. Daniel was sure he'd carry that lonely sight with him the rest of his life.

After riffling through the anglers' magazine in five seconds or less, he pulled his laptop case from beneath his seat and looked about the large room. In the far corner, to the right of a broad bank of windows, sat a workstation. He slung his bag over his shoulder, picked up his coffee and took it over.

His first thought was to call Annie. In the eight days since she'd arrived at his front door, they had been together every workday, and unless one or the other of them had another obligation, every night, too. And he wasn't weary of her company, either—a bloody first in the life of Daniel Flynn.

No, she'd not yet given him in writing what he knew they both wanted—to the point of sleeplessness and odd lapses of attention. She'd captured his interest completely.

Annie was well-read, lovely and had a fine wit. Of course, she still turned that wit on herself more than he'd like to hear, but it seemed to happen less each day. Another miracle, considering that just now, Donovan's offices were as tense and ugly a place to work as Daniel could imagine.

She'd be at her desk soon, sugary coffee drink and a stack of papers in front of her. Daniel pulled out his cell phone and was about to hit the autodial button when the clerk at the desk began calling out more names. Now, that background noise would be hard to explain away.

He set down his phone, leaving it switched off, and instead plugged his laptop into the communications port so kindly provided by the hospital. In moments, he was on the Internet and sending his Annie a greeting.

DANIEL HAD GONE missing in action. Oh, he'd told her last night that he'd be on the road today. No specifics, of course. The guy could sidestep questions with a skill that Annie found both admirable and annoying.

As she walked to her office, frozen mocha in one hand and briefcase over her shoulder, she began to realize how much she counted on him to cut the tension at work. Even Sasha, who had already informed her grandpa, uncles and dad of her plans and thus was the happiest person in the building, didn't have the same effect as Daniel's smiles and jests. Of course, Sasha didn't look at her in quite the same sexy, it's-gonna-be-sooo-good way that Daniel did, either.

Annie had become addicted to the thought of making love to her Irishman. She also accepted that when it happened—maybe even tonight—it would be no mindless fling and that she'd pay a major emotional price for taking this next step. Still, as far as risk/reward analyses went, she knew she'd come out ahead.

Humming to herself, she turned the corner and nearly collided with Rachel. Since they didn't bother speaking anymore, they traded glares. Their allegiances in the Donovan battle of the titans were clear and opposing. Annie wondered if Evil Queen Rachel had been fitted for the consort's crown, just in case Richard actually managed to boot his father to the curb. She hoped like hell Rachel would hold out for real diamonds. It would take a boatload of carats—and a really tight and favorable prenuptial agreement—to make up for bedtime with hair-flapping Richie.

Once she'd settled in at her desk, Annie checked her business e-mail. She found some stuff from the benefits department, a few follow-up answers from the design team she was meeting with today and about twenty too many forwarded jokes and chain letters. She moved on over to her private account. There, she hit double gold: an e-mail from Daniel and one from Paul Housden, Elizabeth's New York contact.

Saving pleasure for last, Annie opened the e-mail from the corporate recruiter.

"Holy..."

She couldn't even think holy *what*. She'd sent the

guy her résumé last Wednesday, after getting Lizzie's blessing. Housden had already shopped her, and wondered if she'd be available the week of July twelfth—three weeks from now—for initial interviews. At least now she knew she didn't need the additional glamour of having set up the international franchise agreement to get her foot in the door. Buffing her résumé to a hard, glossy shine appeared to have been enough.

Though Housden didn't give company names, one interview would be with a brokerage house, working as an analyst specializing in the food services industry. It seemed a little dry for Annie's taste, but dry might not be so bad after living through World War Donovan.

The next potential spot was in-house for a restaurant conglomerate, which Annie figured was ripe with the potential of seeing her current unhappiness amplified. The final interview the recruiter mentioned was the Holy Grail of jobs, as consultant to an accounting firm's food services and franchise clients.

She knew that an initial interview was far from an offer, but at least she was now a woman with possibilities. Best yet, each potential job was sexy enough that even her overachieving family would have to take notice. Grinning like an idiot, Annie printed the e-mail, then deleted it from the company's system. She'd call Housden from home at lunchtime—after she shopped for a new interview suit that didn't smack of suburbia.

Annie tucked the e-mail into her purse, then started to prepare for her early afternoon meeting with the Ars/Ullman design team. Damn, but life was getting good again.

BY TEN IN THE MORNING, Daniel had checked his e-mail a dozen times and still had nothing back from Annie. He felt so bloody caged and cut off from civilization.

Even Eva's early arrival had done little to pacify him. She'd tried her best, bringing muffins and such from the local bakery. She'd also had the sense to mostly leave him alone, instead badgering the reception clerk for any updates on Hal.

Just past noon, a doctor in drab green scrubs entered the waiting room. "Family of Hal Donovan."

Eva and Daniel rose. After a quick introduction and recap regarding Hal's new stent, the doctor said, "It's doubtful that we'll be letting Mr. Donovan go in the morning. He's running a higher fever than we'd expect to see after a procedure like this."

"Do you know how much longer he'll be here?" Eva asked.

"A guess is the best I can do. We'll be watching closely, but you can figure that Mr. Donovan will be here until some time late Thursday."

Eva frowned. "Can we see him soon?"

"A nurse will come get you."

They thanked the doctor, who quickly left. Daniel returned to his computer.

Two more days. Being dishonest with Annie hadn't sat well in the first place, and now it was damn near choking him. His grand plan had been to drive home tonight, then back to the hospital in the morning. Living two doors down from Annie posed a problem. If Hal was to be delayed, Daniel could hardly keep slinking in and out of town under the cover of darkness.

"Eva," he said to Hal's secretary and likely lover, "do

you know anything about hotels in this area? I'm thinking I need one."

AT THEIR PARENTS' last-minute request—which was actually more of a demand—Annie and Elizabeth returned to the family home for a special dinner that
night. Somewhere along the line, Annie's mom had gotten it in her head that Annie loved *katsu don,* which was
essentially the Japanese version of breaded and fried
pork cutlets plopped on a bed of rice.

Annie actually viewed the dish as fat-coated lead on
a big bed of naptime, especially the way her mom pre-
pared it. But since it was nice of her mom to think of her
at all, she had learned to stomach the meal in silence,
then go home and sleep off the results.

Tonight's *katsu don* wasn't the only bomb settled on
the Rutherford sisters. Annie and Elizabeth had barely
slipped off their shoes and sat in their parents' tatami
room when Max and Alison announced that they'd
both decided to retire at the end of the next academic
year. They were chasing their dream and moving full-
time to Kyoto.

"So far?" Annie winced at just how whiny she
sounded. She might be kissing thirty, but a needy nine-
year-old still lurked beneath the surface.

"With everybody's schedules, it's not as though we
see much of each other anyway," her father said. "We'll
just have to learn to keep in touch by e-mail. Your
brother does a fine job of it, you know."

E-mail! Damn. She'd never gone back to her personal
account to read Daniel's message. Between coming to
an agreement with the Ars/Ullman pub design team,
visiting the corporate kitchen to see how her chef was

faring with menu ideas and spending every unfilled minute angsting over even the potential of New York interviews, she'd totally forgotten that the note waited.

With luck, Daniel would have explained why he'd turned off his phone for the day, forwarding all calls to voice mail. She'd left two messages after leaving the office for the day, mostly for the thrill of hearing the cadence of his voice while listening to his "away" recording. Yes, she was totally obsessed.

"Annie...*Annie?*"

"Um, yes?" It seemed that her family's conversation had moved on without her.

"Elizabeth says you'll be traveling to New York soon to interview for a new job," her father prompted.

"That's the general plan," she replied, then took a cautious sip of her sake.

"But New York? You don't like New York," her mother said.

"Just like the T-shirt says, I heart New York, Mom." *It's* katsu don *I can't stand.*

"Darling, you can't tolerate the place. Do you remember how you cried at the Metropolitan Museum of Art?"

At least she'd pinned the memory to the right offspring. "I was seven and lost, okay?"

"Regardless. Have you been there since then?"

"Of course I have." No need to mention that it had been a theater trip during her sophomore year of college. She'd researched plenty since then and knew what she was doing. "These are incredible opportunities. I'm lucky to even get the interviews."

Her father shook his head. "I have my doubts, Annie. That city seems awfully large for you."

Annie pushed back her plate and set her chopsticks on their rest. "Dad, I'm nearly thirty and haven't exactly been living in a vacuum. Do you think that for once, you and Mom could just be happy for me?"

"The question, Annie, is whether you're happy for yourself."

Score one for parental profundity. Annie tossed back the rest of her thimbleful of sake and tuned out for the duration.

Once she was sprung from her parents' place, Annie headed straight home and to her computer. While she'd been receiving lectures, one e-mail from Daniel had grown to two. The first was the miss-you kind of stuff that made her smile. The second erased that smile in a nanosecond.

Daniel was joining Hal for three days of fishing in the wilds of northern Ontario. His cell phone would be out of range for all but bear and moose. He promised to e-mail from the closest town, if he could, and think of her often.

Nice, but Annie could read between the lines. She'd been abandoned for a string of fish.

DANIEL DIDN'T KNOW a donkey's arse about fishing, except that he likely could have caught a legion of the buggers in the nearly-a-week he'd had to keep extending the excuse to cover Hal's hospital stay. He supposed he was lucky that Hal had chosen a fictional locale from which Annie wouldn't be expecting a souvenir. And Hal was lucky that it was no more than a nasty virus on top of too many years of cigars that had held him in the hospital's care. One thing was for certain, Daniel was off cigarettes for good.

Saturday night, he'd stayed with Hal at his house not

far from the club where they'd had breakfast a few weeks back. This morning, he'd left him in Eva's capable hands and borrowed Hal's car. It was a lazy Sunday morning as he drove Hal's Mercedes toward Cobblestone Court. The driving was going well, too. He was nearly accustomed to this wrong-side-of-the-road nonsense.

Tucked in the back seat was the dartboard sent by Seán. He'd also talked to his brother yesterday. James was back home. It seemed the dispute between Da and James had centered on whether James Joyce had been a wordy old bastard in need of a good editing, as James claimed, or a master of prose, as Da asserted. Daniel laughed just thinking of the insanity of it all. Only in the Flynn family…

Instead of pulling into his drive, Daniel parked in Annie's. He couldn't wait a second longer to see her. He bounded up the steps, rang the bell and waited, then waited some more.

The door opened to the town house the next stoop over, and scruffy-looking Garth, whom Daniel had crossed paths with once or twice, stepped out.

"She's not home," the man said.

"So I'd noticed."

"She left earlier."

"I see," Daniel replied, wondering just how many ways one could state the same thing. "Thanks, then."

Garth shifted from one grotty sandal to the next, looking as though he wanted to say something else. Daniel didn't give him the chance, instead heading down the steps and over to his own stoop.

Inside, the answering machine on his otherwise bare kitchen counter was blinking. Daniel pushed the button.

"Hi, it's me, and it's Sunday morning." He smiled at

the sound of Annie's voice. "If your plane hasn't been delayed or the pilot cornered by a bear or whatever you have left to hold you up today, you'll find me at Hal's pub-to-be. Come see me, okay?"

Daniel turned heel and returned to his car. He intended to see every last bit of Annie Rutherford.

ANNIE HAD CAUGHT episodes of *Monster House* and *Monster Garage* while getting her reality TV fix, but now she was living "Monster Bar." She had to admit that it gave her kind of a rush, seeing how much had changed. Only a few days had passed since the State Street Donovan's had been shuttered, and already the place was gutted. Carpets and tile had been ripped up and clean new subfloor laid. Walls were stripped to the studs in some places and to bare drywall in the rest.

She was about to check out the kitchen when the sound of the front door opening stopped her. The glare of the incoming sun concealed the visitor's features, but Annie knew by the man's height and lean shape—not to mention the pounding of her heart—that it was Daniel. She pulled together a casual attitude to mask the fact that she'd happily tackle him to the bare floor.

"Catch a lot of fish?" she asked as he strolled closer. He carried a pretty sizeable flat package under one arm.

"Enough," he replied.

Annie hazarded a step closer, which was about as much as she could risk without flinging herself at him. She knew she should give him some grief over his disappearing act, but it was hard to stay ticked at a guy who wrote e-mails filled with talk of passion and touching and all the good things she'd been craving for so long.

"So what's in the box?" she asked. "Not the fish, is it?"

"An early pub-warming gift." He walked to the bar, which was still intact, if empty, and set down the box. Annie came over and watched as he used a key to cut the tape sealing the package.

"It's a thing of beauty, isn't it?" he asked once he'd pulled back the box's flaps.

"It's...um...a dartboard." A very, very used dartboard, to be more exact. Daniel apparently fell on the frugal side when it came to pub-warming gifts.

"The finest dartboard ever," he said. "I bought it when I was eighteen and it's been hanging in Flynn's ever since."

"So what's it doing here?"

His smile was brief but definitely not lacking in impact. "I was feeling the need to see a piece of home." He began to walk the perimeter of the naked room. "This will do," he said, then hung the board from a nail that was protruding just far enough. He walked back to the bar and unwrapped two sets of darts from the paper they'd been rolled in.

"Ever played?" he asked.

"No, but I get the general idea of the game."

"Good, then. First we play for a kiss." He handed her three red darts and kept three blue. They were heavier in Annie's hand than she'd imagined. If she wasn't careful, she could do some real damage with these babies.

Daniel walked three paces from the board, then appeared to measure his distance.

"Close enough," he said. "Come stand by me and line yourself up."

The standing-by-him part sounded good.

"Now focus on the middle of the board and let one sail."

"Okay."

How hard could this be? Annie closed her left eye and aimed for the center of the board. Her dart, however, had another location in mind. It bounced off the wall and landed on the floor.

"Again, but this time get more snap to your wrist and point to where you want the dart to go as you release."

This time at least she hit the board, even if the dart didn't stick.

"Better."

The third time was the charm, more or less. Annie gave a hoot as the third dart landed in the outermost ring.

"Grand, love," Daniel said. "Now watch."

He'd thrown his darts before Annie could even blink. All three were far inside the spot of Annie's piddly dart.

"Show-off," she said.

"Just trying to impress."

She laughed. "Consider the job done. Now here's your kiss." She rose on her toes and pressed a kiss against his cheek.

"That's it?"

She hadn't seen such a look of deprivation since booting Garth off the nookie-train. "There's the possibility that I'm a poor loser." Or that she'd just thought of a better game.

"That there is," he said as he gathered the darts, including Annie's strays.

She walked back to the bar, where she'd earlier unrolled a set of schematics for the new pub. Next to them was a pad of yellow sticky-notes that she'd been using to mark her questions on the drawings.

"So have you any plans for the day?" Daniel asked, all casual-guy charm.

She glanced over at him. "I have an idea or two."

He sent a dart flying then asked, "Anything that might involve, say, a written request?"

She was thinking more in terms of a demand. Annie peeled the protective back sheet from the sticky-notes and set it aside. On the first square beneath, she wrote two words just under the exposed adhesive backing— *my bed.*

"Writing me a note, are you?"

"Go play, Flynn. Your game might be slipping."

"Now don't be angry because I beat you. Practice, Annie, that's all you need."

Oh, she intended to get some practice.

"Just keep playing," she said, jotting on the backs of each of the little yellow squares. She glanced over and caught him spying. "No cheating, either." She cupped her free hand so that it barricaded the notepad from prying Irish eyes.

"You're a hard woman, Annie Rutherford."

He sent a dart flying. It landed just a smidgen outside the outer ring of the bull's-eye.

"I'm learning," she replied.

Annie concentrated on finishing off the last of the notes. She heard two more darts hit the board, each making an authoritative thump. On she wrote. When she was done, she joined Daniel.

"You're the sporting type, right?"

"It depends on the wager," he replied.

"Oh, this one you'll like…guaranteed." She strolled to the dartboard and plucked the three darts he'd thrown and handed them to him. Then she returned to the board and began sticking the yellow squares of paper to it. "On the back of one, and only one, of these notes you'll find that written demand you've been asking me for."

"Will I now? And what would I be finding on the rest?"

"Nothing nearly so entertaining, I'm sorry to say." Satisfied that the board was covered, she pocketed the rest of the notes. "So here's the deal…hit the right note and we spend the day together in my bed. Hit the wrong one, and…" Annie finished with a regretful shrug.

"Make that a brutally hard woman," he complained, but Annie saw the light of competition in his eyes. Giving first the board and then her a considering look, he hefted a dart in his hand. "So you're telling me that on the back of only one of those dozens of papers are the words *my bed*, and I've three tries to find it?"

"Yes."

"And I'm to trust this grand event to luck?"

"Right again."

"Damn good thing I'm Irish, then, isn't it?"

"Ooh, good point. I hadn't figured that into the equation." Annie moved in front of him and settled her hands on his shoulders. "Turn around."

"Why?"

"I don't want to make this too easy on you."

"You're not. You have my word on it."

"Backing down from a challenge, Flynn?"

He laughed. "More like turning away from it." He reversed his position and Annie followed. "Here we go…three over my right shoulder."

One…two…three. Annie watched as the darts flew in rapid succession. When he was done, she released the breath she hadn't quite realized she'd been holding.

"Let's have a look," he said, strolling to the board. "Which do you think I should pull first?" he asked in a conversational tone, as though they were discussing the range of color for the slate floor in front of the bar.

"Move it along, Flynn."

"I'm betting you'd have chosen a spot away from the middle. After all, you've got plenty to gain from this wager, too." He reached for a dart in the lower right quadrant of the board, but then paused at the last instant. "But you know I'm good, don't you, Annie?"

She suspected that he was going to prove to be beyond good. "Do you plan to pull one before morning comes?"

Daniel plucked the dart closest to the center of the board, bringing with it the slip of paper it had pierced. He read it and his smile grew.

"Your bed, Ms. Annie."

"Impossible." She held out her hand for the note. "You're bluffing."

But he'd been honest. The slip truly read *my bed*. He'd hit a one-in-two-dozen shot. She tucked the note into the back pocket of her shorts. She'd never kept a scrapbook…until now.

Daniel settled his hands on her arms and looked down at her. Annie could see the beginnings of concern in his expression.

"Only if you're ready," he said.

She went up on tiptoe and settled a fast kiss on his mouth. "Beyond ready. How about you?"

In answer, he took her hand and hurried to the door.

After Annie and Daniel left, one of the remaining yellow notes parted from the dartboard and lazily fluttered to the ground, leaving the message *your bed* facing up. Coincidentally, those words could be found on the back of each paper still clinging to the board.

Annie Rutherford was no fool, except for love.

14

ANNIE HAD NEVER underrated sex. Based on her fairly limited scope of experience, she'd been sure that she enjoyed it as much as the next girl. But now that she had Daniel thoroughly, perfectly naked, she realized that those earlier lovers had just been warm-up acts for the big event.

A trail of his 'n hers clothes marked the path from Annie's front door to her living room. Daniel and she were breathing as though they'd sprinted all the way from State Street, instead of having driven. His mouth was hungry against her breasts, her stomach—everywhere he could reach. She was just as greedy, kissing and touching and marveling at how damned beautiful this man was. The skin of his throat was smooth under her lips and his gasped words were fire under her skin.

Annie let her fingertips glide down, then up, the length of his erection. Need slammed into her even harder when she imagined taking him into her body. She couldn't believe she'd denied herself this pleasure for even a day.

Daniel folded his hand over hers and asked for more. Annie gave, but still hungered. She knelt before him and took him into her mouth, something she'd never before done without a certain amount of persuasion—okay, sometimes begging—from her partner. He allowed them only a moment of hot pleasure before drawing her upward and folding her in his embrace.

His broad hands gripped her bottom and brought her even closer to him—not that she had any intention of moving away.

"You, Annie Rutherford, are witty, wise and beautiful, and I need to be inside you *now*."

He took her to the couch. Annie was too scattered to do more than stand there as he pulled away the back pillows and sent them flying. Next, her reading stack was unceremoniously relocated to the floor.

"Good enough," Daniel said.

"Perfect," Annie corrected, then stretched out on the soft chenille surface. She'd regretted getting sucked into the oversized furniture craze, but now it seemed to be the smartest move she'd ever made.

Second smartest, she amended as Daniel slid his hands up her inner thighs. She opened her legs, inviting him to touch more. He did, until she was pretty much mindless with pleasure. When he drew away from her, she murmured a protest.

Daniel knelt, one hand braced on the couch's back. "Where'd I leave my wallet?"

She waved a hand in the general direction of the door. "That way…hurry."

He was up, gone and back before she'd had time to do much more than stretch once and breathe deep, trying to get oxygen to a body working overtime.

Annie watched as he fitted on a condom, the moment oddly intimate and intrusive all at once. She held out her arms to him. He filled them, settling his weight above her. He kissed her then, deeply and with a hunger that echoed her own.

Annie reached between them, closing her hand around his erection. "Now. Please."

"Now," he agreed, and she guided him until he'd just begun to enter her. They pressed deeper into the cushions, and she settled her hands against his upper back. Slowly, carefully, he began to push his way in.

Overwhelmed, she gasped.

Daniel hesitated. "I'm not hurting you, am I, love?"

She arched her pelvis upward and wrapped her left leg around his hips. The action brought him the rest of the way home.

Daniel smiled. "That answers that."

He began to move, and any initial discomfort Annie had felt was long gone. In its place was sheer pleasure.

She'd expected their first lovemaking to be a little goofy, a little awkward, but she'd been wrong. They fit together wonderfully. She wanted him too much to worry about whether she was becoming too demanding or too loud or too *anything* other than desperate for release. She didn't even care that she could hear Garth pounding on the other side of the living room wall.

Daniel lifted his head, sending a distracted look in the direction of the sound. "What's that?"

"Ignore it," she ordered, then wrapped her legs even snugger to show that she meant business. Her breath came in little hitches, and she could feel even her toes begin to curl as Daniel flexed in and out with sure intent.

"God, Annie," he gasped as her inner muscles began to tighten around him.

She cried his name as she reached her peak. When he came, she held him close, new waves of pleasured shock eddying through her. As they rested, exhausted and replete, Annie knew she'd been right—she'd never be able to let go of Daniel Flynn with any amount of grace.

DANIEL LAY IN THAT perfect Zen state of contentment—half awake, half dreaming, and with a mind ready to wander.

He'd made love to Annie in the living room and in her bed. Next, they'd engaged in a little food love play in the kitchen, where a now one-eared donkey pepper shaker had fallen to the floor, victim of their enthusiasm. After that had come the shower, and then her bed once again.

Somewhere along the line, the sun had left and stars had replaced it. He wasn't sure whether it was yet Sunday or if Monday had crept up on them. His selfish and futile wish was for another month of Sundays like the one they'd just shared.

Annie lay snuggled against him, dozing. He slid one hand over the lush curve of her hip, an act that got an unexpected rise—and not out of him. She sat bolt upright, nearly knocking his jaw with the top of her head.

"Daniel, we need to go back to the pub."

"What?"

"The pub," she repeated, pushing her hair from her face. "Now."

Daniel glanced at her alarm clock, but couldn't make out the first two numbers. They seemed to be blocked by the Space Needle shaker set he'd bought her. If it weren't so damned ugly, he'd be truly touched.

Ah, touching. Now there was a better activity to be pursued than a mad chase through dark Ann Arbor streets. He sent one hand venturing for the silky skin of Annie's thigh.

She swatted him away. "I'm not kidding! We need to get there before the crew."

This was pushing devotion to an employer a wee bit far. "Why?"

"I left some papers behind."

"Then they'll be there after sunrise, too."

"But I don't want anyone else seeing them. They're kind of private."

"Private, how?"

"You know all the other yellow notes on the dartboard?" she asked in a voice he'd describe as sheepish, except he'd never quite understood the origin of the term. It wasn't as though sheep ever sounded sheepish.

"Mmm-hmm," he said.

"Well, they aren't exactly as empty as I led you to believe. They all say *my bed*, and I really don't want an entire construction crew leering at me for the next month."

Daniel laughed. And here he'd been worried about shooting blanks, so to speak. "You, Annie Rutherford, are a cheat. And I'm damned lucky you are." He settled her against the pillows and kissed her once for her sharp ways, then once again, because she felt so damn right under his mouth.

Finally, she smiled up at him. "A girl's gotta do what a girl's gotta do."

"Stay here, love. I'll go gather your notes."

"You'd do that?"

"For a price. I'm expecting repayment on each and every one of them."

She frowned. "I don't know, Flynn. That's a little steep."

It took him less than an instant to see her game. "And you're a damn poor bluffer."

"Hey, I got you in the pub, didn't I?"

"You did," he admitted as he rolled from the bed. In

fact, it was beginning to seem that she now had him in every way that mattered.

Daniel bent and kissed his sharp Annie one last time, then readied to go collect a plump stack of IOUs.

ANNIE OPENED THE pencil drawer of her desk and peeked at her cache of yellow slips. Ten days…ten notes. She briefly touched the top one and smiled. They were like her own little security blankie, something she could go to when the stress of the Donovan control battle made office life intolerable.

Each note brought a memory, since Daniel had been creative in his means of delivery. She'd received one in a box of Fourth of July sparklers he'd left propped against the iced tea pitcher in her refrigerator. Another had arrived attached to a checklist during the final tasting for the pub's menu. Today's had been in the bottom of the coffee mug she kept on her desk.

At first, she'd been concerned that he would run out of notes before they ran out of days together. Then, one evening, as he'd been writing at her kitchen table, she'd spotted the remaining stock in his laptop case. If all else failed, she could keep replenishing the supply.

Oh, she understood on a flat-out logical level that the notes weren't what drew him to her bed, and that they had nothing to do with the passage of time. Still, maintaining the fantasy helped her stave off the sick feeling that threatened when she thought of Daniel's departure. Or her New York trip.

Annie closed her desk drawer, leaving comfort behind. She knew she was doing the right thing, pushing ahead with these interviews. Yet it was taking every ounce of her willpower and positive thoughts to feel good about the process. Daniel had even offered to come along and keep her company, a major sacrifice considering how un-in-love he was with Manhattan. She'd refused. Having him there whispered too much of wrapping up this never-to-be repeated time in her life.

"Guess what?"

Annie glanced up to find Sasha in her doorway.

"I don't know. What?"

Bottle of mineral water in hand, her friend strolled in, then settled into a guest chair. "While you've been off dabbling in intimate international relations, my life's become a children's book—*Sasha Gets a Second Mommy*."

"No way."

"Yup. Dad called me at home last night and told me to pencil in the third weekend in September for a wedding. Of course, being Dad and assuming everyone can read minds, that's all he told me." She took a swig of her water. "Since I'm not dating anyone right now, I figure he's got to be referring to himself."

"So it's Rachel, huh?"

Sasha set her bottle on Annie's desk and gave her an appraising look. "How'd you know that?"

This was why she'd make a miserable spy. She'd totally forgotten that she'd never shared the suck-face in the parking garage incident. "I, uh…kind of saw them together last month."

"Do tell. And you didn't mention this to me, why?"

"It was the night I met you at Armando's. I didn't want to put both of us off our food."

"Right."

Sasha wasn't buying it, and Annie couldn't blame her.

"I'm really, really sorry. I was just trying to be a good friend. Hey, I still owe you a grovel. Want it now?"

Sasha shook her head. "I'll pass. But a little warning would have been helpful, you know? I just about gagged on my drink when they showed up together at Gramps' Fourth of July bash."

A bash which Daniel and Annie had opted out of, in lieu of a more underdressed, private celebration…complete with sparklers.

"Yeah, that would have been a shock," she said to Sasha.

"I'm sure I'll adjust to having a stepmom who's two years older than I am. And in the meantime, can you be away from your Irishman long enough to go cheap-and-insincere engagement gift shopping with me tonight?"

Annie scrambled for a nonpathetic excuse. "We…I—"

Sasha laughed. "It's okay. I understand." She stood, and before leaving, raised her water bottle in a salute. "Here's to true love."

Long after Sasha had split, Annie ruefully considered one question. Out of all the words her friend could have chosen—say, *lust*, for example—why did she have to pick *love?*

DANIEL WASN'T SLEEPING well, and hadn't for days. Tonight, after making love to Annie in celebration of yellow note fourteen, he simply lay there and watched her sleep, one more image to tuck away in his memories. His contract with Hal expired in a matter of weeks, and though the older man had made noises about extending it, Daniel had no desire to do so.

Annie would be leaving for her New York interviews tomorrow after work. He had no doubt that she'd interest one employer or another. He also had no doubt that once an offer came, she'd take the job. He did doubt that she'd be happy.

Still, he couldn't blame her for grabbing at the chance. Continuing employment with the Donovans would be about as appealing as marching barefoot across a field of broken glass.

Daniel crossed his hands behind his head and gazed up at the darkness. It was time to consider what he'd do next. Perhaps a few months in Clifden would suit him well. And after that, there was always helping his friends get a start in Belize, or even some travels for no particular purpose—once his favorite reason of all. Nothing appealed, though. No place seemed more tempting than one close enough to smell the flowers-and-vanilla scent of Annie's hair.

She stirred, then sighed, wriggling farther under the covers. He tried—and failed—to imagine her living out of a tent or traveling by decrepit bus on a South American mountainside. She knew herself well, his anchored Annie, and now he was the one having trouble letting go.

MONDAYS WERE GENERALLY ugly, but one glimpse at the morning paper had told Annie that this particular one was going to be hideous. In fact, her flight to New York this evening would be a regular day at the spa when compared to what she faced now.

She and Daniel walked the march of the doomed into the boardroom. All of the Donovans, including Sasha, were already gathered around the large table.

"Can I get you two anything?" Eva D'Onfrio asked as they passed her sentinel's post at the door.

"A double shot of whiskey, up, would be grand," Daniel said.

Once they were seated, she brought them each a coffee, instead. Annie cupped her mug, hoping to take some of the chill from her hands.

From his front-and-center spot, Hal stood and smacked down the *Focus on Business* section of the *Washtenaw Press*.

"Pizza Dynasty Done?" howled the headline.

Annie had already read the article, as had everyone else in the boardroom. Though specifically stated nowhere, the piece implied that Hal Donovan was no longer capable of running his empire.

"Who would like to claim responsibility for this?"

Richard cleared his throat, then said, "I will."

Annie shot Sasha an I'm-so-sorry-your-dad's-a-rat look and hunkered down in her bunker.

"You've dragged our business into the public?" Hal shouted.

"You left me no choice." It was small comfort that Richard was mighty low on swagger-factor today.

"Bull."

"The next step is a shareholder suit, and I'll file. Believe me, I'll file," Richard said. "You're not the only one who's put his life into this place. I started helping out when I was fourteen. That's nearly forty years ago, dammit. I can make this company more. I *want* to make it more."

Hal started to speak, but then stopped. An odd look passed over his face. He sat down hard and gripped the edge of the table with both hands.

Duane, who was to his right, leaned closer. "Dad?"

"It's nothing…just feeling funny." He settled his hand over his chest and coughed. "Heart's not beating right."

Annie stood and grabbed for the phone in the middle of the table.

"What are you doing?" Hal asked, his usual crimson flush replaced by chalky whiteness.

"Calling 9-1-1."

"Hang up," he ordered, though not with his usual bullish authority. "We're enough of a spectacle today."

"Get over it," she said to Hal, then asked the operator for medical help. "I think he might be having a heart attack."

"It's not a heart attack. No arm pain. No shortness of breath." He stood. "Look, I'm fine."

"For God's sake, Hal, sit down," Daniel said. "You're not even a month out of the hospital for heart trouble. Do you think we're going to let you stroll to your office and smoke a damned cigar?"

Sasha had gone to kneel beside her grandfather. She tried to loosen his tie, but he pushed her hands away.

"Heart trouble? Is this true, Gramps?"

"It was minor...not worth mentioning."

"He had an arterial stent inserted. Eva and I were there," Daniel said.

Color washed from Richard's face, leaving him nearly as white as his father. *"What?"*

Daniel gave the Donovans the whens and wheres of the event. For once, they responded without the standard hurling of recriminations, focusing only on Hal.

Annie, on the other hand, was losing it. It was all too much for her to absorb—her fear for Hal, the running-rabbit pace of her own heart and the unsettling feeling that Daniel had played her. He'd lied about where he'd been while this surgery had taken place and failed to share the news with her later. Annie deserved to know.

For all of Hal's quirks, he was more than just an employer to her. Soon after Hal had been hauled out, complaining to the medical technicians that he could walk, she quietly slipped away.

HAL HAD GONE TO the hospital with Eva and a full clan of Donovans to watch over him this time. That, at least, was as it should be. Daniel sat in his office, waiting for the phone to ring even though he knew it could be hours yet before they had any news on Hal's condition.

He swiveled his chair around and looked out the window at the neighboring building's window, which simply reflected the same back at him. That caged feeling had begun to overtake him, the one that had already chased him from Tibet to the Amazon, from freelancing for magazines to standing on the working side of a bar. Frustrated, Daniel turned back to his desk and tried to think of some way to break the tension that would make a right bastard of him, if he let it.

Annie walked in, looking nearly as knotted and out of sorts as he felt.

"I take it you weren't in Ontario in June?" she said.

No dancing about the issue for her.

"No," he replied.

"You could have told me the truth."

"I honored Hal's privacy, Annie, just as he asked me to."

She sat in a chair opposite his desk. "And doing so involved a lie."

"Let's talk about this later, when things have calmed," he suggested.

"Daniel, it's enough for me to be worrying about Hal

and wondering if I should delay my trip tonight. Can't we at least get through this?"

"Fine, then," he said, rubbing at his hammering temples.

"Do you agree that you lied to me?"

The walls seemed to grow closer. "If you want to take the hard view of it, I suppose I did. Not willingly or happily, and knowing that it would come back to bite me." It was a grudging admission, but what more could she expect?

"Okay. Then putting aside the hurt to me, don't you think his family had the right to know?"

"Only if he chose to tell them. He was scared, Annie. He's growing old and he's never let his family see him as he really is." Daniel rose and came around to her side of the desk. "I didn't mean to hurt you. If he'd fallen ill or even shown the slightest sign of relenting, I would have told you and the others."

"What would have been the harm in confiding in me right away?"

He chose his words carefully. "I've been watching the way Richard and his jackal brothers have been behaving. I can't fault Hal for protecting his flank. If I'd said something to you and word had leaked, I'd be a poor friend, indeed."

"I see," she said in a voice so tight that it had to hurt. "So instead you decided to judge me as one."

"You're being unfair."

"Am I? Or are you?" She turned her face away from him, but not so quickly that Daniel didn't see the beginnings of tears.

Nothing like a weeping woman to make a man feel cornered. "Annie, I—"

She stood. "I'm sorry. You were right, maybe later is a better time." She was out the door before he could object, not that he'd planned to.

He'd deal with this later. Much, much later.

Daniel returned to his desk, closed his eyes and imagined himself someplace far from the Donovan empire, someplace friendly, open and warm.

JUST PAST SIX THAT evening, Annie sat at her gate in Metro Airport's McNamara Terminal. Her flight didn't leave for another hour and a half, and she'd already been at the airport long enough to buy a book, stock up on junk food and pace the long arm of the building from beginning to end. Airports remained among her least favorite places, but they had pulled ahead of Donovan's headquarters.

At midafternoon, Sasha had called Annie's office with some good news. Hal's heart episode had been a harmless case of tachycardia, probably brought on by stress. He was fine now, but considering his history, they were going to keep him overnight anyway. After thanking Sasha for the update, Annie had tried to get word to Daniel, but he had gone. His cell phone went unanswered, too. An hour later, Annie had left for the airport. Distracted as she was, sticking around work would have been just for show.

Annie regretted the way she'd walked out on Daniel, regretted that she'd even criticized him to begin with. Bottom line, the choice had been his to make. Weighing loyalties was no job for outsiders, and like it or not, she was on the outside of Hal and Daniel's friendship.

In the mood to munch, Annie hauled her carry-on

bag onto the seat next to her and unzipped the outside pocket. The chocolate-covered pretzel rods she'd picked up looked pretty tasty. Of course, she could always go the healthier route and try the trail mix, never mind that it was about forty percent candy-covered chocolate.

As a minor sop to her conscience, Annie settled on the mix. She dug into the bag, trying to avoid the stuff she could live without. She was about to pop the first handful into her mouth when she froze. Enough was enough. She wasn't even hungry, dammit. Annie dumped the trail mix back into its bag, then tossed the whole thing into the trash can at the end of her row of seats.

"Better," she said to herself. Maybe she hadn't gotten rid of the chocolate-covered pretzels, but this was a step in the right direction.

Then Annie took her next one—doing as she wished Daniel had done. She pulled out her phone and dialed Sasha. "Three guesses where I am and what I'm doing…"

Annie laughed at her friend's first guess. "No, it doesn't involve a naked Irishman."

But she sure as heck hoped that wherever she ended up once this crazy ride was over, she'd find a way to have Daniel there. And yes, nightly naked, too.

15

By NOON WEDNESDAY, Annie was back in Ann Arbor with a couple less vacation days to her name. The interviews had gone well enough, and New York had been incredible, if a little overwhelming. Maybe, in time, she'd work up a veneer of sophistication and not be so excited by every corner vendor, shop window or celebrity she thought she might have spotted. Or maybe not. That's what was making this choice a total bugger—her lack of certainty. There was one thing she was sure of, though. She had missed her Irishman.

Annie walked up the steps to Daniel's front door. She'd called the office on the way from the airport, and Mrs. D. had told her that he was home tying up a few things. He appeared at the door only moments after she rang the bell.

"Hey," she said. Not quite as up-front as the "I'm so totally in love with you" she was thinking, but there was no point in sending the man screaming into a sunny Michigan day.

Daniel smiled, yet it wasn't quite the full Flynn smile of guaranteed seduction.

"Hey," he said in return.

Annie slipped into worry mode. "Is everything okay? You know I meant it last night on the phone when I apologized for going off the deep end over Hal, right?"

"I know."

He'd felt distant last night, too, but Annie had put it down to projecting her case of nerves onto Daniel. She'd told herself that it wasn't as though she could see his face from New York City or judge what was going on with him. But maybe it was time to start trusting her instincts.

"Would you like to come in?" he asked.

"Sure." She stepped inside after him and nearly fell over a suitcase to the left of the door.

"Business trip?"

"Not exactly. Why don't we have a talk?"

"Sure." She kept her voice level, no easy task when her heart was plummeting to her stomach.

Annie followed Daniel to the kitchen, a telling choice on his part, when his bed would have been the other seating option.

She pulled out a chair, sat, then asked, "So what's up?"

"I'm leaving tomorrow."

"For how long?"

He gave the answer she'd been dreading since that evil *talk* word had cropped up. "For good."

Annie scrambled for a way around his announcement. Finally, she resorted to legalities. "But your contract isn't up for another two weeks."

He took his time answering. "Hal understands there's no more I can do."

What she considered a pretty justifiable case of anger began to spill over. "You mean there's no more you choose to do."

"Annie, you've got the perfect team assembled to get the pub up and running. You don't need me here."

This wasn't about the pub, and it killed her that he'd choose to play it that way. She was no good at this, no good at acting as though he hadn't ripped her heart out.

"So where are you going?" she managed to ask.

"Home for a while, then maybe Belize."

"Why *Belize*?" The question had been automatic, but suddenly Annie realized something. She just didn't care. She held up her right hand, palm out. "Wait, don't answer that. It really doesn't matter why. Belize is just a symptom."

"A symptom?"

"Yes, of your moving-on disease. You can't help yourself, can you?"

Something that might have been either anger or humor briefly sparked in his eyes. "Someone's been reading *Psychology Today,* haven't they?"

He was a master at baiting her, but she'd developed some skills, too. She'd also been watching Daniel Flynn in action for weeks. "Nope, you're not throwing me off this time. I think I finally have you figured."

"Do you now?"

Annie was growing more certain of it by the minute. "You're a regular renaissance man, Daniel. You play the fiddle, write and seem to have some skill in common with nearly everyone you meet. It's all very cool stuff, but it's also finally hit me…. You're good at so many things because you never stick with one long enough to become great. And you know why? Because you're afraid."

He laughed. "That's mad."

"Is it?" She parked her pride curbside and gave him the truth. "And here's the thing…though I'm really, really angry at you right now, I love you, and I think you probably love me, too."

He looked down at the table, then back at her. "Annie—"

"Hang on, I'm not done. I figure the odds are pretty slim on my ever finding anyone else I love this much who loves me back. Daniel, if this is it for me, I want it to be great. I *deserve* great."

"You do," he said.

She had one question to ask before she picked up her pride and moved on. "So what would you say if I asked you stay here in the States with me?"

"You know I can't," he fired back.

"Or won't."

Color had begun to show along his cheekbones. "Let's try it another way, Annie. What if I were to ask you to travel with me?"

"For how long?"

"I don't know."

But she did, unfortunately. "Until you find another distraction. This is what I mean. You won't hang in to find *great*. I love you, but I can't pack up everything I own and just wander the planet with you. I need goals, a purpose.

"Pick something, Daniel, I don't care what. Pick it because you love it and then pursue it with all your heart. Maybe you don't owe me great, but you owe it to yourself."

He ran his hand through his dark hair, which was already disheveled. "We both knew I'd be leaving sometime. Don't make this so difficult."

"But some things in life are difficult, okay? Some things really stink and we have to fight to get through them. But once we do, we end up smarter and better." At least Annie hoped so, because she'd never felt more rotten.

She pushed away from the table and stood. "And

sometimes we even find love. You know, Daniel, I think we really could have been amazing." Since she could no longer hold back her tears, she left.

Silence reigned after Annie's departure. Silence and fury. Daniel had never heard such a pile of stinking garbage as her accusations. He was no dabbler, and no coward, either. He grabbed on to all life had to offer because he could. And he would also leave right now instead of tomorrow. Somewhere was a place free of Ms. Annie's razor-blade pyschocrap.

Half an hour later, as Daniel's cab rolled past Annie's town house, he told himself never mind how it felt at that moment, he wasn't running away. Dammit, he wasn't.

HAL CALLED A MEETING of senior management on Friday. Since Daniel had been true to his word and left town, Annie walked to the boardroom heart heavy and alone. She'd done little over the past forty-eight hours but mourn. She was right about Daniel, and knew that she deserved better, but that didn't make her current situation any more bearable.

"Good morning," she said as she entered the room.

Instead of just Hal and Mrs. D. responding, the Donovan sons returned her greeting, too. Shocked, Annie sat. Maybe she'd somehow wandered into a parallel and happier universe. Her surprise grew as, for the first time in recorded history, a gathering of the Donovans began without the boys sniping at one another.

"First item on the list is the State Street location," Hal said. "Thanks to the hard work of the team that Annie assembled, I've been told that we should be ready to reopen effective August fifth. That date right, Annie?"

She checked her time line. "It is."

"That date will also mark the day that I step a few chairs to the side at this table. You'll notice I didn't say stepping *down*, Richard," he added with a glare at his eldest son from over the tops of his reading glasses.

"My hospital visit shook me up. Life's short, and I'm getting tired of doing the same thing every day. Still, you can't expect me to give this place up. What you can expect is to start seeing a little less of me. That means you, Duane, are going to have to see a little less of the golf course, and that the rest of you are going to have to learn to get along better."

He turned and nodded to Mrs. D. She placed a sheet of paper in front of each of the meeting's participants.

"What you see here," Hal said, "is my proposal for a new division of power."

Annie scanned the organizational chart. It seemed fair, with Hal as Chairman, and Richard moving up to CEO. With the exception of Duane, who remained General Counsel, the others had been promoted. Sasha even remained as Honorary Community Liaison, which suited her perfectly.

Annie looked down another level and found her name. She sifted through her emotions to see how she felt about the possibility of remaining with the Donovans, as a direct report to Richard.

Just as she felt about New York, it seemed…totally uncertain.

Maybe Richard would mellow now that he had the power he craved. And perhaps wedded bliss with Evil Queen Rachel, who Annie knew from Sasha would be retiring to start a family as soon as possible, would be enough to allow Richard to age with grace, too. But did she care?

From Annie's perspective, security and a chunky income were good, but they just weren't *great*. She frowned at Hal's chart as though it was the source of her confusion. She knew better, though. The source was across the Atlantic Ocean and still messing with her mind.

"These are just some thoughts I've been batting around," Hal said. "If anyone has any objections or better ideas, let me know."

He had just announced himself open to compromise! Annie was tempted to dash to the window and see whether a flock of pigs might be flying by.

"I know that, to a person, everyone at this table thought I'd lost my mind when I announced the pub chain." He laughed, a sound Annie hadn't heard in weeks. "It turns out that you were half-right. I don't want a chain and probably never did, except that I don't believe in thinking small.

"It turns out that what I really want is the same thing Daniel Flynn's father has in Ireland—a place to work when I want and to play the rest of the time. Donovan's State Street Pub is a one-of-a-kind item, and I plan to take a personal hand in it. Probably even check on it daily," he added.

He looked at Richard. "You can sit down with your lawyers and decide if what I'm offering is enough to keep you happy. But I'm telling you now, son, it's my final offer."

Richard looked at the paper a moment longer, then back at his father. "I don't need to talk to anyone else. This is fine, Dad. Thank you."

Annie had to glance away from Hal's fleeting expression of relief. Her tears had been far too close to the surface over the past several days and she damn well refused to cry in the boardroom.

"Good," Hal said. "Now, on to the next piece of business...."

Clifden, County Galway, Ireland

DANIEL KEPT LITTLE from his travels other than memories and notes. No souvenirs, few photos...nothing that might draw him back. Why, then, couldn't he let go of *these?*

He shuffled through the square yellow notes he'd pulled from his pocket, each bearing the same message—*my bed*—in Annie's round printing. He'd picked them up then put them back aside countless times since coming home, as though by reading them, he could understand the hold the notes—and Annie—continued to have over him nearly two weeks after he'd left.

"Enough," he muttered, then tossed the notes into the small trash bin behind the pub's bar. Less than a second later, he dredged them out. Fool that he was, he could neither keep nor throw them away.

Just then, his mam popped her head in the front door. "I'm off to run a few errands," she called. "Is there anything you're needing?"

"An exorcism."

She stepped all the way inside and came to the bar. "My hearing must be going, just like your da's. Did you say *exorcism?*"

He should know better than to jest about matters of faith with his mam. "Sorry, just a joke."

"And not in the least funny," she sniffed. "Now, is there anything you really need?"

"There is," Daniel said. "Can you hang on just a sec?"

Without waiting for her answer, he went to the drawer beneath the pub's phone and rummaged through the papers, cards and other bits of semibusiness stuff kept there. Finally, he dug out an envelope. It was crumpled and of indeterminate age, but still fit for the role of exorcist. He addressed it to Annie, took the notes from his pocket and tucked them inside. He didn't plan to think so very hard on why he might be doing this. His mind was too swampy a place to wander these days.

"Would you mind buying some stamps and putting this in the post for me?" he asked his mother.

She took the offered envelope. After she'd read the address, she looked back at him, and Daniel felt again a child under her gaze.

"You won't be delivering this yourself?" she asked.

"I won't."

His mother sighed. "I worry about you, son."

Which was fitting, as Daniel was worried, too. He'd done nothing but occasionally tend bar and consistently turn down friends' offers of a night out since he'd been home. And as for his writing? At this point, he was well suited to write dark, knotted bits of dirgelike poetry, which would please neither his publisher nor himself.

In sum, Daniel Flynn was well and truly blue.

Ann Arbor, Michigan

ANNIE SHUFFLED through her mail and froze at the sight of an envelope bearing foreign postage—Irish postage. Still clutching the envelope, she walked to her office door and closed it.

"Get a grip," she told herself, realizing that her palms had gone from warm to cold and clammy in three seconds flat. Again seated, she opened the envelope and pulled out its contents.

She gazed down at yellow notes identical to those inside her desk drawer. Annie peeked inside the envelope to see if some message had been included, but there was none. She also checked each of the notes to see if anything had been added, and found nothing.

Annie wasn't the witty, wordy type, like Daniel. She'd hated her college lit courses, agonizing over the meaning behind each word in a poem. She figured that authors should just say whatever it was they were trying to say, and get over themselves.

So what the hell had Daniel been trying to say?

Annie lifted her phone and dialed Sasha's extension. "Would you mind coming to see me? Something strange came in the mail."

"So what is it?"

"Just get over here."

"Cool, a mystery," her friend said. "I'll be there in a minute."

While Annie waited for Sasha, she weeded through some old files. Yesterday, she'd given Hal notice. Her boss had been understanding, and even told her that there would always be a place for her at Donovan's. Annie appreciated the sentiment, but given the change in management, she doubted she'd ever take him up on the offer.

Two days ago, she had also received an offer from the New York brokerage house. Because she wasn't certain, she'd asked to have until the end of the week to think about it. If all else failed, she could be doing research and analysis in Manhattan. Granted, it wasn't her dream consultant's job, but it would do in a pinch.

Though it ate at her to admit it, her father had been

right. New York wouldn't make her happy. The urge to hole up there and never move again was as much a symptom of her unsettled state as Daniel's constant traveling was of his.

And she did owe Daniel an enormous debt. Since he'd come into her life, she'd started to see her attributes, not just her faults. The struggles of the past weeks had made her less hungry to satisfy others, yet starved to please herself. Seeking change wasn't wrong. Settling for less than her personal bliss, however, was.

Annie's office door flew open and Sasha dashed in. "Okay, so what's the big mystery?"

Annie slid the notes across the desk. "These came from Daniel. They were kind of a game we played together, and now he's sent them back to me. No letter…no nothing…just these."

Sasha thumbed through the notes, then gave Annie a smile. "I like the games you guys played."

"They were great while they lasted," Annie agreed. "So what do you think this means? Do you think he's just cleaning up loose ends?"

Her friend handed back the notes. "He could have done that by throwing these out."

Annie's heart beat faster. "True. I suppose I could call him."

Sasha shook her head. "That's the chicken's way out. Live big, Annie. You've sat in Ann Arbor long enough. Get back out and see the world."

Excitement and the certainty she'd been lacking for so long began to bubble up inside Annie. She could do this. She knew she could. She smiled at her friend. "I've heard Ireland's nice this time of year…."

Clifden, County Galway, Ireland

"WHAT'S IT GOING to be, Dan? Do we have to come up there and drag you down?" James Flynn bellowed up the stairway that led from the pub to Daniel's rooms.

Daniel supposed at least there would be some sport in being dragged down. He knew that Seán and James together could eventually take him, but then it would be his teenage years all over again, with Mam fussing about how they were going to break everything the family owned and could they not just love each other for one day? He shut down his computer and steeled himself for some well-intended badgering, for Da had called a family meeting.

"I'll be right there," he shouted to the inquisition waiting below.

Daniel left his self-chosen prison and walked downstairs to not four, but five worried faces.

"You've fallen in with an evil lot," he said to Aislinn, who was sitting just close enough to Seán that Daniel's suspicions about their feelings for each other were confirmed.

"I'm worried about you, is all," she replied.

"There's nothing wrong with me that a decade or so of forgetting won't cure."

"And that," Da said, "is why we're all here. It's time for you to quit brooding and do something."

Daniel pulled out a chair and sat. "Look, I know I've been rough to live around since I got home, but I'm pulling out of it."

His mother slid an envelope across the table to him. Daniel opened it and found airline reservations back to Michigan.

"You need to finish this, son," she said.

He tucked the paper into its envelope. "Ah, but it's not that simple. Annie won't have me. She says I'm too afraid to grab what I want, and she doesn't mean just her."

"Smart girl," James said. "I'm thinking she has a point."

He'd have told his brother to shut his fat gob, except James was right. As Annie had been.

Daniel had concluded early this morning that he didn't like the down and mournful world of a sad Irishman. He was sick of sitting alone at night, contemplating his navel and his general arse-headedness. And he was dead sick of not being able to write. He knew the time had come to leave the cave, take a risk and get on with life. He even had an idea or two on where this life would lead him. Of course he still needed detail sufficient to persuade a vice president of long-range planning to fall in with his scheme.

Daniel pushed back from the table.

"Not so damn fast," said Seán. "We're not through with you."

"But I'm through with doing nothing."

He rounded the bar and pulled open the jumbled supply drawer beneath the phone. There waited a notepad, the same kind as Annie had once used to brilliant success. Daniel dug a bit more and pulled out a pencil.

"Quick," he said to his family, "give me all the jobs you remember me having."

As they called out the likes of "bartender," "tour guide" and "restaurant critic," Daniel jotted each one on the back of a square yellow slip of paper.

He was feeling in the mood for a game of darts.

On the road to Clifden

WAS SHE DOING the right thing in coming to Daniel, or was she making it too easy on him? After hours of travel, did she look as if she'd been wrestling with a goat? Annie sure felt that way. She glanced in the rearview mirror, then quickly looked back as a car's horn sounded.

Dammit! She'd drifted to her usual side of the road, which made her total accident bait in Ireland. Annie swerved back to the "wrong" side and mouthed a truly contrite sorry to the driver of the car she'd nearly run off the road. And it wasn't as though there was much of a side to the road here. It slipped off from low, jagged rock into boggy green.

At least there was little risk of getting lost on this part of her journey. Exactly one major route led from Galway City to Clifden, unlike her circuitous drive from Shannon Airport to Galway. She should have just sucked it up and taken the extra commuter flight, as her travel agent had suggested. But no, she'd taken the chicken's land route.

Of course, she had no idea what she was going to do once she found Flynn's Pub. Looking like a total boob was a recurring theme in all possible scenarios. She'd never chased a guy ten feet, let alone across an ocean.

She drove past the fairy-tale beauty of Kylemore Abbey, which, she'd read in a travel guide, was once a home built by a man for the woman he loved. Now it was a convent, tea room and private girls' school. Maybe nothing in life turned out exactly as planned, but that wasn't necessarily a bad thing.

Far before Annie was ready, Clifden appeared. She knew from Daniel that the pub was on the far reaches of the town, nearly to something called Sky Road. Sitting on the edge of the Atlantic, Clifden was larger than just the smattering of houses and shops she'd somehow expected. It was pastel-pretty, too.

Annie could almost picture herself living here one day in the far-off future. She'd have a house on the hillside, with the mountains behind her and a view of the water. Never mind that, given her current semi-unemployed state, she'd have to hit the lotto to afford this life of leisure. Or that she wasn't too sure about her welcome from Daniel.

Trusting herself to fate, she slipped into an open spot along the narrow road and parked. Scrutiny of her reflection in the rearview mirror confirmed that she looked like an inductee into the undead. Annie dug through her purse and dredged out a hairbrush, mascara and a freebie lipstick sample that had been floating around down there forever. When she was satisfied that she'd done about as much good as possible, she exited the car.

A warm and humid breeze kissed her skin. The sun peeked from between postcard-perfect fluffy white clouds. It was in all ways an idyllic day, except she didn't know where she was going.

"Excuse me," she said to a woman walking with a baby in a stroller. Or pram. Or whatever the heck they called them in Ireland. "I'm looking for Flynn's Pub?"

"Head straightaway to the next block, then turn right." The woman hesitated, then added, "They won't be open for another hour at least, you know?"

Annie nodded. "Okay, thanks."

Since she had nothing else to do in the coming hour except question her sanity, she walked to the pub and tugged at its red front door, fully expecting it to be locked. Instead, it flew open, leaving Annie staggering. Once she'd collected herself, she stepped inside. The light was a little dim to her adjusting eyes, but she still saw Daniel lined up in front of a dartboard. Nearby was a group of people, some of whom looked very much like him.

Everyone turned and looked at her. Okay, maybe this wasn't such a hot idea. She took a step toward the door, but then recalled that she'd promised herself to live big, as Sasha had decreed. And that involved grabbing the one thing in life she was one hundred percent sure about.

Annie drew in a nervous breath, then announced, "I, Annie Rutherford, am wise, witty and beautiful. I'm also hoping you've figured out that you can't live without me, Daniel Flynn."

Her voice had enough tremor to it to set off an earthquake, but she was pretty sure she'd gotten the message across. So why wasn't he moving?

Daniel looked like he was trying to form words, but none seemed to be coming out. In that instant, she silently filled in the blank with "What the holy hell are you doing here?" and "You look familiar. Have we met?"

Finally, he spoke. "You took a plane all the way here by yourself? That's hours and hours, Annie."

She nodded, then wiped the tears that seemed to be messing with her hastily applied makeup. "I noticed. It went pretty well, too, except for the guy next to me asking the flight attendant to take away my pen because I was making him crazy."

Daniel tossed the darts he held in one hand to the closest table, not even noticing when they rolled to the floor. Then she was in his arms, sweet warmth washing through her as she rediscovered that sense of being home.

He kissed her long and hard.

"I love you, and how I've missed you, too," he said low into her ear, which was enough to really make her sob.

Someone tapped her on the shoulder. Through her tears, Annie caught a hazy image of a pretty girl around her age with brown curly hair.

"Take these," the girl said, pressing some tissues into her hand.

"Thanks."

"Your manners, Daniel," prompted a woman who could only be his mother.

Daniel introduced Annie to his family, who were warm and welcoming enough that she almost forgot what a nervous mess she was. Eyes cleared, Annie looked around a little.

"What's on the dartboard?" she asked Daniel.

"I was, uh, making some career decisions."

Annie's joy expanded until she was forced to grin, just to let some of it go. "Interesting method."

"One of my favorites," he replied, then took her hands. "After leaving you, I had plenty of time to think, Annie. Much as it pains me, you were right. I've been pushing aside the one thing I do best. I'm going to be a writer, love, which means I'm nearly guaranteed to be poor."

"But you're a brilliant writer," his brother James said. "And didn't I see they gave Bertie Ahern's daughter a fine advance for her work?"

Daniel glanced over at his family. "Can't you go find something better to do than watch us?"

"Probably not," said Seán, earning a smack on the shoulder and a "Don't be a total fool" from Aislinn.

Mrs. Flynn managed to persuade the lot of them as far as the bar, leaving Annie and Daniel about twenty feet of privacy.

"If you want to live in New York, I'll do it," Daniel said. "In fact, on the backs of those bits of paper decorating the dartboard are all the day jobs I thought I might be able to stomach while writing at night." He shook his head. "The oddest thing is, I'm finding I can stomach the thought of a lot, so long as you're with me."

She wanted to kiss him again, but knew if she did, she'd never stop. "It doesn't look like I'll be moving to New York. In fact, I think I've kind of decided to go into business for myself. I got my first client the other day."

"Client?"

She nodded. "The brokerage house I interviewed with. I turned them down for a permanent job, but offered them a contract deal. I'll be tracking franchise trends in the food and beverage industry."

"No New York? Then where will you be?"

"Other than coming here, I haven't thought that far ahead," she admitted. "But so long as there's Internet access, I'm golden."

He grinned. "Then I'm guessing the world's ours."

Annie watched as Daniel walked to the dartboard and began pulling down the yellow notes.

"Grab a pencil," he said. "Since we're free to roam, let's write down all the places we want to see together."

"Slow down, Flynn. I'll travel with you when you can't hold still anymore, but my salt-shaker collection, not to mention my clocks, all have to live somewhere."

"That's the idea, love. Ann Arbor," he said. "Or Amsterdam or Athens. Write down the places and three darts at a time, we'll shop for a home."

She nearly stopped him, but then accepted that he needed this. Change was a gradual thing. If it took some wandering for Daniel to see that he'd already found his way, she was game. Well, game as long as he held her hand on each flight and never once complained about the volume of luggage she required.

Paris she wrote on the first slip and *Clifden* on the next.

"Really?" Daniel said, reading her Irish choice.

"Could be."

Once they were done writing, Daniel stuck the notes on the board.

"Come here," he said. "Let's do this together."

Annie gathered the darts and walked into the circle of his arms.

"Over my shoulder, right?" he asked.

"Of course."

Taking her with him, he turned away from the board. Daniel let the darts fly, and Annie watched as they landed. One seemed to be square in center of the board.

"Double bull, I'm guessing," James opined.

"Only single, at best," said Seán.

"Shall we?" Daniel asked her, nodding toward the dart.

She shook her head. "Later."

The "where" of their future didn't matter nearly as much as when it started. To the cheers of his family, she kissed her Irishman. Annie Rutherford was officially in like Flynn.

SILHOUETTE *Romance*®

In a
Fairy Tale
World...

Six reluctant couples.
Five classic love stories.
One matchmaking princess.
And time is running out!

Playing matchmaker is hard work— even for royalty!

The only way to tame a shrewish socialite is to kiss her senseless, at least according to scruffy but sexy marine biologist Bradford Smith. And now that he's accepted a makeover from Parris Hammond, the barbs—and sparks— are flying! This frog is more man than she's ever met...but can he truly become her prince?

HER FROG PRINCE

by **Shirley Jump**

Silhouette Romance #1746
On sale December 2004.

Only from Silhouette Books!

Visit Silhouette Books at www.eHarlequin.com   SRHFP

HARLEQUIN® *Blaze*™

Members of Sex & the Supper Club
cordially invite you to a sneak preview of
intimacies best shared among friends

When a gang of twentysomething women
get together, men are always on the menu!

Don't miss award-winning author

Kristin Hardy's

latest Blaze miniseries.

Coming in...

August 2004 TURN ME ON #148
October 2004 CUTTING LOOSE #156
December 2004 NOTHING BUT THE BEST #164

Advance reviews for *Turn Me On:*

"A racy, titillating, daring read..."—*WordWeaving*

"Hot, sexy and funny...Ms. Hardy has a definite winner
with *Turn Me On.*"—*Romance Reviews Today*

"Kristin Hardy begins a new trilogy with a great appetizer...
this is one hot book...think *Sex and the City* meets L.A."
—*All About Romance*

www.eHarlequin.com   HBS&S

If you enjoyed what you just read,
then we've got an offer you can't resist!

Take 2 bestselling love stories FREE!

Plus get a FREE surprise gift!

Clip this page and mail it to Harlequin Reader Service®

IN U.S.A.	IN CANADA
3010 Walden Ave.	P.O. Box 609
P.O. Box 1867	Fort Erie, Ontario
Buffalo, N.Y. 14240-1867	L2A 5X3

YES! Please send me 2 free Harlequin Flipside™ novels and my free surprise gift. After receiving them, if I don't wish to receive anymore, I can return the shipping statement marked cancel. If I don't cancel, I will receive 2 brand-new novels every month, before they're available in stores! In the U.S.A., bill me at the bargain price of $4.24 plus 50¢ shipping & handling per book and applicable sales tax, if any*. In Canada, bill me at the bargain price of $4.94 plus 50¢ shipping & handling per book and applicable taxes**. That's the complete price—what a great deal! I understand that accepting the 2 free books and gift places me under no obligation ever to buy any books. I can always return a shipment and cancel at any time. Even if I never buy another book from Harlequin, the 2 free books and gift are mine to keep forever.

131 HDN DZ9H
331 HDN DZ9J

Name _____ (PLEASE PRINT)

Address _____ Apt.#

City _____ State/Prov. _____ Zip/Postal Code

Not valid to current Harlequin Flipside™ subscribers.

Want to try two free books from another series?
Call 1-800-873-8635 or visit www.morefreebooks.com.

* Terms and prices subject to change without notice. Sales tax applicable in N.Y.
** Canadian residents will be charged applicable provincial taxes and GST.
All orders subject to approval. Offer limited to one per household.
® and ™ are registered trademarks owned and used by the trademark owner and or its licensee.

© 2004 Harlequin Enterprises Ltd.

FLIPS04R

e♦HARLEQUIN.com

The Ultimate Destination for Women's Fiction

For **FREE online reading,** visit www.eHarlequin.com now and enjoy:

Online Reads
Read **Daily** and **Weekly** chapters from our Internet-exclusive stories by your favorite authors.

Interactive Novels
Cast your vote to help decide how these stories unfold...then stay tuned!

Quick Reads
For shorter romantic reads, try our collection of Poems, Toasts, & More!

Online Read Library
Miss one of our online reads?
Come here to catch up!

Reading Groups
Discuss, share and rave with other community members!

For great reading online, visit www.eHarlequin.com today!

INTONL04R